Another line? Really? line, too, not some vague little shadow.

Georgie got up, her legs like jelly, and walked out of the bathroom, sank down onto the bed and stared blankly at the test strip.

How could she possibly be pregnant? Dan had said it was a tiny tear, and she and Mark had tried for years. How could she be? Unless they'd just been incompatible, but even so…

She slid a hand down over her board-flat tummy. Was there really a baby in there? Dan's baby?

Please, no.

Please, yes!

But…

She'd have to tell him. Not yet, though. It might have been a fluke. She'd do another test in a while.

And then another one, until all the tests were used.

Four couldn't be wrong.

She started to cry, great tearing sobs welling up from deep inside her where the pain she'd hidden for so long had festered like poison, and then they died away, leaving only joy.

She was having a baby, the thing she'd always dreamed of and had given up hoping for.

Dear Reader,

The joy of writing is inventing a heartbreaking scenario and finding a way out of it for your hero or heroine. It's even better to do it for both of them!

Dan's lost a baby; Georgie's been betrayed and never conceived. So what do you do to an obstetrician and a midwife? Give them twice as much joy—but when it's a high-risk pregnancy, it plays to both their fears. Will the babies make it? And will their relationship survive? Read on to find out, but have your hankie ready!

Caroline x

THE MIDWIFE'S
MIRACLE TWINS

———

CAROLINE ANDERSON

HARLEQUIN
MEDICAL
ROMANCE

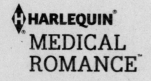

HARLEQUIN®
MEDICAL
ROMANCE™

Recycling programs
for this product may
not exist in your area.

ISBN-13: 978-1-335-40907-2

The Midwife's Miracle Twins

Harlequin Enterprises ULC
22 Adelaide St. West, 41st Floor
Toronto, Ontario M5H 4E3, Canada
www.Harlequin.com

Printed in U.S.A.

Caroline Anderson is a matriarch, writer, armchair gardener, unofficial tearoom researcher and eater of lovely cakes. Not necessarily in that order! What Caroline loves: her family. Her friends. Reading. Writing contemporary love stories. Hearing from readers. Walks by the sea with coffee, ice cream or cake thrown in! Torrential rain. Sunshine in spring or autumn. What Caroline hates: losing her pets. Fighting with her family. Cold weather. Hot weather. Computers. Clothes shopping. Caroline's plans: keep smiling and writing!

Books by Caroline Anderson

Harlequin Medical Romance

Hope Children's Hospital

One Night, One Unexpected Miracle

Yoxburgh Park Hospital

Risk of a Lifetime
Their Meant-to-Be Baby
The Midwife's Longed-For Baby
Bound by Their Babies
Their Own Little Miracle
A Single Dad to Heal Her Heart
From Heartache to Forever
Tempted by the Single Mom

Healing Her Emergency Doc

Visit the Author Profile page
at Harlequin.com for more titles.

Huge thanks to Carol, who fed me cake and helped keep my midwife on the straight and narrow, and to John, as ever, for his endless patience. Love you.

Praise for
Caroline Anderson

"What a delightful story…. Overall, Ms. Anderson has delivered an emotionally animating and entertaining read in this book…the romance was nicely detailed."
—*Harlequin Junkie* on *From Heartache to Forever*

CHAPTER ONE

'Do YOU NEED a man?'

Absolutely not, and particularly not the owner of the low, soft voice with a hint of laughter that came from behind her, but she'd exhausted all other options, so she stopped wrestling with the lid of the peanut butter and turned to face him.

He was propping up the door frame of the ward kitchen, arms folded and looking sexier than a man had any right to look in scrubs, and as she met his eyes a lazy smile tipped his mouth and tilted her heart sideways.

He had heartbreaker written all over him and under any other circumstances she would have run a mile, but right now she was too tired and hungry to refuse. She thrust the jar towards him.

'Do you know what? I've tried everything else. Knock yourself out.'

The smile tilted a little more, and he shrugged

away from the door frame and twisted the lid off with ridiculous ease.

'It's all in the wrist action,' he said, that sexy mouth twitching, and she rolled her eyes and relieved him of the jar, stifling her smile.

'I think you'll find it's brute force, but thank you anyway.'

His lips twitched again. 'You're welcome. My brute force was happy to oblige,' he said, and she stuck a spoon in the jar and put it in her mouth before she could make another smart retort.

He gave a startled laugh and pulled a face. 'Good grief, you must be desperate,' he said, but she was past caring.

'Hungry,' she mumbled, her mouth all stuck up with the peanut butter, and he laughed again, this time with a hollow ring.

'You're not alone. If I didn't loathe it, I'd grab a spoon and join you. Someone nicked my lunch out of the fridge. I'm Dan, by the way. Dan Blake.'

As in Daniel Blake, their new consultant? She nearly choked.

'Georgia Seton, aka Georgie,' she said, throwing the spoon into the washing up bowl and sticking out her hand. 'I'm a midwife.'

'I'll look forward to working with you, then, Georgia Seton,' he murmured as his hand grasped hers in a firm yet gentle grip that sent interesting tingles up her arm.

Well, that was one way of describing them. Dangerous was another. Their eyes met and locked, his a cool grey framed by dark lashes and the crinkle of laughter, and her heart hitched in her chest. She ignored it. She wasn't ready for that kind of interesting. Not now, not ever.

He dropped her hand and she turned away from those mesmerising eyes, plunged herself wrist-deep into the washing up bowl in the sink and washed the spoon—and her hands, to get rid of the feel of his warm, firm grip as much as anything.

'Back into the fray?'

His voice, like dark, melted chocolate, teased her nerve endings again. 'Hopefully not,' she said lightly. 'Paperwork on my last delivery, then home for something proper to eat before I keel over. And with any luck I won't be three hours late again today.'

He snorted. 'Good luck with that. They broke me in gently with a nice simple elective list today, then chucked in a couple of emergencies just to mix it up, so I'm only running an hour late so far. I thought I'd come and introduce myself to whoever's here on the labour ward on my way home, see if there's anything useful I can do before I leave. Apart from opening jars.'

That made her smile. 'Good idea. They'll appreciate it. And thank you again for rescuing me.'

'You're welcome. Just don't dream up a crisis before I get out of here.'

She gave a hollow laugh at that. A crisis was the last thing she needed tonight. She'd been running on empty for hours. 'I'll do my best.'

She flashed him a smile, squeezed past him in the narrow kitchen and caught the scent of his skin as her nose skimmed by his chest. No way. She was not interested.

Absolutely not...

'Ah, Georgie, there you are. Can you do me a favour? Kat's had to go home, she's got a migraine, and we've got a primip who's walked in with a slight bleed and everyone else is tied up. She's just moved here, so we don't have a hospital number for her yet but she'll have her handheld notes with her. Room four. Her name's Susie.'

Her heart sank at her team manager's words. She'd only just finished writing up her last delivery, and she was about to go home. Or not, by the sound of it...

'Is there really nobody else, Jan?'

'No. I'm really sorry, but the night shift'll be on soon and it's probably nothing to worry about.'

Don't say that!

She sighed and closed her eyes. 'OK. I'll go and see her.' She shut the file and headed for what Jan seemed to think might be nothing to worry about. Which had probably jinxed it utterly.

She went into the room and found a young woman sitting cross-legged at the top of the bed with her eyes closed, a man, presumably her partner, sitting beside her stroking her hair back off her face.

They looked up as she closed the door, and she smiled at them. 'Hi, my name's Georgie, I'm a midwife and I'm going to be looking after you. You must be Susie?'

'Yes, and this is Rob. He's my partner.'

'Hi, Rob. Good to meet you. Susie, I understand you've had a bit of bleeding. Is that right?'

She nodded, her hands stroking her abdomen in a gentle rhythm, her eyes a little worried. 'Yes. I think I've just been overdoing it with the move, but I thought I should get it checked out. It was just a few spots, but my placenta's low so I thought it was best.'

The shrill scream of alarm bells rang in her

head. A low placenta. Fabulous. Jan had definitely jinxed it.

'OK, well, let's have a look at your hand-held notes and see what they've got to offer.'

Susie shook her head, her eyes welling with tears. 'I don't know where they are. I put them down somewhere and I can't find them because the house is in chaos—we've only just moved. My section was due next Friday and I was going to come in tomorrow to see someone but we didn't know we were going to be moving so soon and it was such a rush and now I'm bleeding...'

Great. It just got even better.

'Don't worry, we'll sort it out,' she said calmly, handing Susie a tissue to blot up her tears. 'We'll need your name, date of birth, hospital number and so on so we can contact your old hospital and get the notes sent over. Rob, I wonder if you could go to the desk out on the ward and give all that information to the ward clerk while I look at Susie? And tell her I said it's urgent. Is that OK with you both?'

'Yeah, sure,' he said, and dropped a kiss on Susie's forehead. 'I won't be long.'

She smiled at him, and Georgie picked up her pen. 'Right, Susie, as we don't have any notes for you I need to take some details and then do a quick scan to see what's going on. Did they give you a grade for your placenta previa?'

She gave a little shrug. 'I don't know. They never said.'

'Has this happened before? Any spotting, pink discharge, anything like that?'

She shook her head. 'No, nothing. I've been fine and I've felt OK till now, but…'

'Do you know your due date?'

'Yes. The twenty-fifth of August. I'm thirty-seven weeks and five days. I don't know if it's significant but I've been having a few—not contractions, really, I don't think, but sort of tightenings?'

The alarm bells got louder. 'Braxton Hicks contractions, probably. That's quite normal. It's your uterus toning up ready for the main event, but tell me if they get worse. Right, I need to do a scan so we can see what's going on, but before I do that I just want to put this clip on your finger. It monitors your heart rate and your oxygen saturation, so it'll give me an idea of how you're doing. Have you had any blood pressure problems?' she asked, strapping on the cuff.

'Not as far as I know.'

Well within the normal range, and her sats were ninety-eight per cent. All good so far.

'Right, let's have a look at this baby. Have you felt it moving today?'

'Oh, yeah. It wriggles all the time, and sometimes it jerks.'

'That's probably hiccups, it's quite common. Could you pull your top up, please?'

Susie hitched up her top and wriggled her jeans down, and Georgie could see at a glance that the baby was sitting very high. She laid her hands on the taut swell of her pregnant belly, feeling the smooth curve of the baby's back, the hard jut of its little bottom up under Susie's ribs, the sharp point of a tiny heel on the other side as it stretched, but the baby's head wasn't engaged in her pelvis, even though it was head down. She pressed gently on the baby's bottom, trying to coax it down, but it didn't move at all.

Not good news. Her placenta must be very low.

'OK, let's have a listen to baby's heart, shall we?' she said, and moments later the steady swooshing sound filled the room.

One hundred and fifty-two beats a minute, which was spot on. Small mercies. 'Well, that's all good. Right, let's do an ultrasound scan now, so we can find out a little bit more about what's going on in there and get a look at this placenta.'

'Do you think that's caused it?'

She smiled reassuringly, trying not to stress her. 'It might be, but you're both doing well at the moment so I'm not worried for now.'

'Oh, I'm having one of those things again. The Branston Whatevers.'

Georgie paused the scan. She could see the tightening of her uterus under the skin, the changing shape of Susie's bump, and judging by the look on Susie's face it wasn't a Braxton Hicks.

'Breathe, Susie. Nice and light, quick little pants and an outbreath, again and again until it eases. That's lovely. Well done.'

By the time it had worn off Rob was back in the room, and he settled himself back beside Susie, holding her hand and looking worriedly at the screen as Georgie ran the transducer over her lower abdomen.

She felt her heart kick up a notch as the image appeared on her screen. The placenta was very low, spanning the area of the uterus that was starting to thin and stretch. Grade Three, and she was in the very early stages of labour, but the baby's heartbeat was strong and steady, and so was Susie's. For now.

She took a photo of the image on her phone,

wiped away the gel and smiled at them both. 'OK, Susie, your uterus is starting to pull up at the bottom where your placenta is, so we're going to have to deliver the baby now. The first thing I'm going to do is take some blood and get that off to the lab, then book Theatre for you, OK?'

Her eyes widened and she reached for Rob's hand. 'Is my baby all right?'

'Yes, it's fine at the moment. Nice strong heartbeat, which is what we want to see, and you're OK for now, but your placenta is very low, which is why you've had that bleed, so I'll get a surgeon to have a look at it and get the ball rolling, OK?'

They nodded blankly, and she put a cannula in her hand, took all the necessary bloods and handed Susie a gown.

'I won't be long. Could you undress and put this on while I'm gone? I'll only be a minute.'

She slipped out of the door and hurried to the work station. 'Can you get these off to the lab now for urgent cross-match and group and save, and page the on-call registrar for me, Sally? I've got a mum with a placenta previa who needs an emergency section.'

'She's helping Samira with a breech—she's only just gone in. Patrick's here somewhere?'

The F2 who'd been with them a week.

'Damn. No. I need someone more senior. She's contracting. Is Mr Blake still around?'

'I thought I told you not to dream up a crisis?'

She turned, and he took one look at her face and the smile faded from his eyes. 'OK, what is it?'

'Grade Three placenta previa, twenty-five-year-old primip. Thirty-seven plus five weeks. They've just moved and she's lost her notes, so we have no records for her, but she's had a slight bleed and she's starting contractions. The move was a bit rushed, I gather. Here, I took a photo of the scan.'

He glanced at it, and his mouth tightened a fraction.

'OK. She needs an emergency section. Have you told her?'

'Yes, and she's stable at the moment, but it won't last. Do you want to check her now?'

'No, I trust you and I've seen enough. Go and prep her for surgery and get her consented, I'll kickstart this and come and join you.'

'OK. I've done bloods for cross-match and group and save.'

'Good. Thanks.'

She left them to it, his voice following her.

'Can we get a crash section team on standby, please, and a Theatre ready asap? Theatre One should be free. They were cleaning it when I left. And activate major haemorrhage protocol.'

The door closed softly behind her, cutting out their voices, but she was relieved to hear him sound so controlled and in command. And he trusted her judgment.

Letting out a quiet sigh of relief, she went over to them and perched her hip on the bed and took Susie's hand. 'Right, I've had a chat to Mr Blake, one of our consultants, and he wants to do your Caesarean section now. He's going to pop in and talk to you in a minute, but in the meantime I need to fill in the consent form and I'd like to put you and the baby on a monitor, just so we can keep an eye on things until Theatre's ready.'

She shook her head. 'I'm so sorry. This is my fault. The move was so difficult, it went on too long and I knew I should have contacted you but I didn't have time, and now I've done too much and I can't believe this is happening—'

Georgie squeezed her hand. 'Susie, stop. This is not your fault, and you're here now, you're safe, and we'll look after you. Don't worry. It'll soon be over, and you'll make a quick recovery and your baby will be OK and you can all settle down in your new home.'

She put her on the monitor and everything looked fine. So far, so good. She rapidly filled in the notes, assembled all the things that would be needed, drew up the consent form, talked Susie through all the possible things that could go wrong, gave her a pen to sign the form and then handed her a tissue when she started to cry.

'I really can't believe this is happening. I thought I'd be OK.'

'You are OK,' Georgie said firmly. 'We just want to make sure you and your baby stay that way.'

She printed off a host of labels for all the things that would need them, and then glanced up to scan the monitors for the hundredth time. Nothing drastic in the way of change for either mother or baby, but they were both subtly different, and she felt a flicker of unease.

'How are you feeling, Susie?'

'Not great. I'm having one of those Branston things again and I feel a bit woozy,' she moaned, her face wincing, and Georgie checked the monitors again and felt the flicker of unease ramp up a notch. There'd been nothing to worry about a moment ago, but now the baby's heart rate had dropped a little, and Susie's blood pressure was down slightly while her heart rate was rising. Not much, but enough, and Georgie was reaching for the alarm button when she heard the door open behind her.

'Hi. How are you doing?'

Dan Blake's steady, reassuring voice came from behind her, and she turned and met his expressionless eyes.

'Minor decels,' she said quietly, knowing Susie wouldn't understand that she was talking about the baby's falling heart rate, and his eyes flicked to the monitors, an unreadable expression in them as he took in the non-reassuring trace.

'Are we good to go?' he asked.

'Yes, all done, she's consented. She's ready.'

'Good. Thanks.' He looked beyond her and smiled, his face all calm reassurance now.

'Hi, Susie. I'm Daniel Blake. I'm one of the consultants here, and I'm going to be looking after you.' He stood at the foot of the bed, keeping the monitors in view as he spoke to them. 'I understand Georgie's told you that we need to deliver your baby now by Caesarean section?'

'Yes. Please get it out safely.'

'That's what I'm here for,' Dan said, and it sounded oddly like a vow.

Georgie took her hand and gave it a gentle squeeze.

'It's OK, Susie. You don't need to be scared. We're looking after you. I just need to get another line in, and we'll take you straight up to Theatre as soon as they're ready for you.'

'I want my mum. Can we wait for her? She's on her way.'

Dan shook his head, his voice gentle but implacable. 'No. I'm sorry. We need to move fast, and I know it will all seem like a bit of a rush, but it isn't, it's all under control, we do this all the time. Trust us, Susie. You're in the best place.'

Georgie saw Susie's shoulders droop in resignation. Thank goodness.

'OK, sharp scratch coming,' she said, and as she finished inserting the port, Susie's eyes widened.

'Oh. I think I've wet myself,' she said weakly, just as the alarms on the monitors started to beep. There was a dark, spreading stain on her gown, her blood pressure fell off a cliff, and the baby's heart was racing.

'Right, let's go,' Dan said crisply, and knocked the brakes off the bed as Georgie hit the alarm button again and it all kicked off.

Rob leapt to his feet, his eyes wide with fear, and Georgie unhooked all the leads and tried to reassure her terrified patient and her equally terrified partner as the team leapt into action and they ran for the lift.

Someone was holding the lift doors open, and when they opened again seconds later she was whisked into the waiting Theatre, Rob running with them to the doors, his hands knotted together in fear.

'Don't let her die. Please don't let her die.'

'It's OK, Rob, we've got this, it's what we do,' Dan said quietly, giving his shoulder a quick squeeze, and they wheeled Susie through into the theatre suite and handed her over to the anaesthetist, the doors swinging shut behind them.

There was no time to scrub, just a massive dollop of hand sanitiser up to the elbows, then gowns and gloves and they were in there with the hastily assembled team, Susie already anaesthetised and draped, a nurse on each side of her squeezing in O negative blood, a TXA infusion going into another vein to stop the bleeding, oxytocin to contract her uterus, the neonatal team hurrying in around them as Dan picked up the scalpel and glanced at the anaesthetist.

'Are we good to go?'

'Yes, but don't hang about.'

'I won't. Right, let's get this baby out.'

It was the fastest section she'd ever witnessed, and it wasn't subtle, but in moments he'd pulled out the floppy, grey baby boy and handed him to Georgie. She cut the cord and handed him straight to the waiting neonatal team and turned her eyes back to Dan's hands.

He'd removed the placenta, but it wasn't intact, and he was searching for the missing fragment while the inexperienced F2, Patrick, was trying his best with the suction.

'BP's falling. Fifty over thirty-five,' the anaesthetist said.

Dan swore, clamped both hands around her uterus and held it firmly while they squeezed more blood into her.

'OK. It's picking up. Seventy-five over fifty.'

'Right, I'm going to have one more go, and if I can't find this bleed in the next few seconds she'll lose her uterus,' he said grimly. 'Suction, please.'

He let go, but the suction failed to keep up and she could feel the tension in the room.

Jo, the registrar joined them, hurrying in to take the suction off Patrick, who was clearly panicking. Jo tried to clear the field for Dan to see.

'Don't you dare die on me,' he said under his breath as he struggled to find and stem the bleed, but for a few seconds Georgie really thought she would. Either that, or lose her uterus and with it the chance of any further children. And there was still no sound from the direction of the neonatal team.

'How's the baby?' Dan asked, as if he could read her mind.

'Alive but unresponsive.' The terse reply came from the other side of Theatre, and he swore again.

Then a tiny cough, so small they nearly missed it, and then the merest hint of a wail, and she saw the tension pour out of his shoulders.

He closed his eyes for a moment, sucked in a deep breath then started again, finding the last scrap of placenta and removing it, giving the oxytocin a chance to do its job. The flow stopped, her blood pressure picked up and once he was satisfied it was all right he nodded and started to close.

Georgie felt the tension drain out of her, and her eyes prickled with tears.

'I thought we were going to lose them both,' she said softly, her voice shaking.

'So did I and we could have done. You should have called me sooner.'

He was blaming her? 'This is not my fault, Mr Blake,' she said quietly but firmly. 'I'd only been in there a very few minutes, and as soon as I'd scanned her I came straight out to alert Theatre. It's not my fault.'

'No, of course it isn't. Sorry. Bit of a sore point. I apologise.' He met her eyes, his filled with an expression she didn't really understand. Something to do with that sore point? She gave a tiny nod of acknowledgement.

'Good. Accepted—but for the record, I don't overlook things.'

'I'm glad to hear it,' he murmured, and carried on suturing, layer by layer, the concentration pouring off him in waves.

'Right, that's her uterus and muscle layers done. Jo, can I leave you to finish off, please? I want to go and talk to her partner.'

The registrar nodded, and they left her closing the skin and went out to give Rob the good news.

He wept with relief when he was told they'd both made it so far. Georgie could empathise with that, she was pretty close to it herself, and she didn't think Dan looked too great, either.

'Right, I need a shower and then I'm going home, and I think you ought to do the same,' she told him after they'd checked on Susie in Recovery, and he nodded.

'Good idea. Thank you for your help.'

'You're welcome.'

* * *

She spotted him in the ward kitchen ten minutes later, and she was shocked. His hands, rock steady while he'd been operating, were trembling so hard he could barely hold the glass of water in his hand, and his face was as white as his shirt.

'Are you OK? You're shaking.'

'I'm fine. Just low blood sugar. I'll be OK once I've eaten.'

'Are you diabetic?'

'No, I just haven't eaten since breakfast, but I'll be fine. I'm sorry I bit your head off,' he added, and she decided to cut him some slack.

'I'll let you off this time. Want some peanut butter or will it choke you?'

He gave a short grunt of what might have been laughter. 'I think I'll pass. I'm going home. It's only a twenty-minute walk and I've got food in the fridge. I'll be fine.'

He didn't look fine, far from it, and it didn't sound as if he had anyone at home to feed him, either.

'I've got a better idea,' she said. 'I've got a massive chilli in the slow cooker, a fresh loaf of tiger bread, and I live just round the corner. Literally five minutes and you can be eating it. What do you say?'

He hesitated, long enough that she knew

just how bad he must be feeling, so she pushed harder.

'I've got a sticky toffee pudding in the freezer. We could crack that out, too. Look on it as a welcome to your new job.'

She saw him buckle, and heaved a silent sigh of relief.

'Sold,' he said crisply. 'Now let's get out of here before anything else happens.'

He wouldn't have made it home.

His whole body was shaking, he felt sick and lightheaded from low blood sugar and a massive adrenaline surge, and underlying it all was a tidal wave of emotion that was threatening to swamp him at any moment.

Of all the things to happen on his first day...

'Right, we're here. Come on in.'

As she opened the door, his nose was filled with the delicious smell of chilli, and he followed her through the hall into the little kitchen.

It was clean, tidy, unassuming—a bit like her, he thought. She'd been calm and unflappable throughout, but with a hint of iron. Like when he'd accused her of not calling him soon enough. She'd put him firmly in his place. He liked that. Less keen on the fact that he'd been so quick to accuse her of incompetence...

She handed him a knife, a board and the loaf of tiger bread. 'Right, you slice the bread while I dish up. And don't be coy with it, I'm ravenous.'

She opened the slow cooker—not massive, but certainly more than big enough for two—and spooned out two huge dollops into bowls while he sliced the bread into big fat chunks.

'Cheese, yogurt?'

'Anything. It smells amazing.'

His stomach growled audibly, and she laughed. 'Here you go. Grab the bread and come on through.'

She led him into the living room at the back of the house and he followed her, his legs like wet spaghetti, and dropped into a chair at her dining table. The chilli was hot and fragrant, and he forked it down as if his life depended on it, mopping it up with chunks of soft, buttery bread until the bowl was wiped clean and the bread was all gone. Then he sat back and offered her a rueful smile.

'That was delicious. Thank you.'

'You're welcome. Feeling better now?'

'I'm getting there. I can't believe someone nicked my sandwich.'

She laughed and got to her feet. 'I can. Sticky toffee pudding?'

'Absolutely. If you can spare it,' he added

as an afterthought, but she'd already walked out with their plates, so he stayed where he was and looked around him, taking in his surroundings for the first time.

It was a typical little modern town house, with the kitchen at the front and the living room behind it running the full width of the house, with French doors that led into the little garden. It was tiny, hardly more than a courtyard, and fully paved, but she'd made the best of it. It was stacked with pots overflowing with colour, and it looked fresh and inviting. His eyes tracked inside again, scanning the artwork on the walls, the choice of furniture, the soothing colour palette with little pops of vibrant colour that echoed the planting outside.

There was a crumpled throw over the back of a sofa, and a magazine lying open on the coffee table, as if she'd just got up and walked away. It was homely, welcoming, the house of someone who cared where they lived.

Unlike him. He didn't really care about anything, not any more. So long as he had a bed to sleep in and a sofa and TV and a kitchen to hold body and soul together, he was OK. It was the garden he cared about, the only thing that mattered to him, because being outside surrounded by nature brought him a glimmer of the peace he yearned.

That and work, only not today. Today was the worst kind of day, the kind that pushed all his hot buttons.

He shut off that line of thought as she came back in with two steaming bowls of sticky toffee pudding topped with a scoop of vanilla ice cream.

'That looks amazing.'

'Don't get too excited, it's not home-made. I tried making it once and it was hopeless, so I buy it now. Comfort food, for the days when it all goes haywire.'

He grunted at that. Haywire was putting it politely.

'I owe you dinner,' he said, changing the subject, and she met his eyes.

'I'll hold you to that. Eat up,' she said, and threw him a mischievous grin that stirred something deep inside him. Something vibrant and sweet and carefree that he'd lost long ago.

He picked up the spoon and turned his attention to something safer.

CHAPTER TWO

THEY ENDED THEIR meal on the sofa, her curled up in her usual corner, him slumped at the far end, the remains of a box of chocolates between them and giant mugs of coffee cradled in their hands. Decaf, although she wasn't sure all the caffeine in the world would keep her awake after the week she'd had.

'So what brought you to Yoxburgh?' she asked him round a dark chocolate truffle, and he picked up a hazelnut caramel and shrugged.

'Luck, really. I was looking for a change, they were looking for another consultant and Yoxburgh has a great reputation, so I just applied. It was a bit of a wild punt, but it paid off.'

'It's quite quiet here.'

'It's fine. I like that.'

I, not we, or he wouldn't be here, not if there'd been anyone with a meal waiting for him. Not that she was about to ask, but he volunteered it anyway in the next breath.

'I don't have anyone else to consider, my parents live near my sister and her family in Scotland, north of Inverness, so it's a long drive or a flight to visit them wherever I live. And I was ready for a consultancy. Why not?'

That surprised her. 'So is this your first?'

He gave a soft laugh. 'Doesn't it show?'

'No. I wouldn't have guessed. That was pretty dramatic with Susie, but you didn't hesitate.'

'There wasn't time to hesitate. It helped that I'd been in the same theatre all day with some of the same people, but it's not the first time I've done a crash section by any means.' His eyes met hers, then flicked away again, their expression unreadable. 'Sadly it doesn't always go so well.'

'No. I was so glad you were there, though, with Jo busy, because there wouldn't have been time to get anyone else.'

'No, there wouldn't. It was too close for comfort as it was.'

'But you saved her. Her and the baby.' She smiled to lighten the mood. 'I'd congratulate you on that again, but it might well swell your head.'

'What, because I did what I've spent years

training for?' He shook his head and gave an odd little laugh. 'Unlikely. And *we* saved her. If you hadn't moved so fast it could still have been very different. And I'm really sorry I called you on that. You did well.'

She smiled at him. 'Thank you—and it's OK, you can stop apologising now, you're forgiven.'

'Thank you.' He was silent for a moment, looking lost in thought, then he sucked in a breath, put his mug down with a little clunk and got to his feet. 'It's time I went home,' he said. 'It's getting late and I've taken enough of your time and your hospitality.'

She followed him down the hall, pausing by the door as he turned towards her with a rueful smile that didn't really reach his eyes.

'Thank you for feeding me. You're a lifesaver, I wouldn't have got home without keeling over.'

'You're welcome. And I'll get my own back. You owe me dinner, don't forget.' She smiled up at him, studying his face at close range, seeing the light change in his eyes.

'I won't forget,' he said softly, and with a tender, slightly wry smile he bent his head and feathered the lightest of kisses over her lips, like the touch of a butterfly's wing.

And then they froze.

She had no idea how long they stood there, eyes locked, neither of them breathing, but then slowly, inch by inch, he lowered his head again and touched his mouth to hers, sipping, stroking, while her breath was trapped in her chest and her heart was beating a wild tattoo against her ribs.

Wow, he knows how to kiss, she thought, and then she stopped trying to think and gave herself up to the moment.

It really was only a moment, and then he lifted his head, his breathing fast, his eyes on fire as they burned down into hers. He dropped his arms abruptly and took a step back.

'I need to go.' His voice was taut with tension, his eyes a little wild, and for a second neither of them spoke. And then...

'You don't have to.'

Was that her? Must have been, there was nobody else there, and for what seemed like an age he said nothing.

Then he let out his breath in a gust and met her eyes again.

'Are you sure?'

His voice was gruff, laden with emotion, and she nodded, suddenly more sure than she'd been of anything for years. And why not? He was alone, she was alone... Why not?

She held out her hand, and for the longest

moment he stared at her, then he took her hand in his and let her lead him up the stairs.

She turned on the bedside light, and the soft glow highlighted her tumbled bedding, just as she'd left it sixteen hours ago. It didn't matter. In a few moments it would be tumbled again, and anyway, right then being houseproud was way down her list of priorities.

She turned towards him, and he cradled her face in his hands. They were warm and firm, gentle, but with—not a tremor, exactly, more the hum of the tension zinging through his body and connecting to hers like a high voltage wire, every stroke of his thumb against her cheek sending shockwaves through her body.

And his eyes—they searched hers intently, looking for what? Hesitation? Regret? So she smiled, and laid her hand against his cheek, feeling the rough rasp of stubble against her palm, curiously intoxicating and reassuring at the same time.

'I want you,' she said softly, and she felt as much as heard his breath hiss out against her hand as he turned his face into her palm and pressed his lips against her skin.

'I want you, too.'

'That's always an advantage,' she said with a smile, and he gave a strangled laugh and she felt the tension go out of him.

He delved in his pockets, pulled out a wallet, rummaged in it for a moment then handed her a foil packet. 'Here. We'll need this.'

She put it down on the bedside table under the light, although there was a pain inside her at the needlessness of it. There was no way he was going to get her pregnant. No way he *could* get her pregnant.

She put the painful thought away, reminded herself that there were other reasons for using protection, and pulled her top off over her head and dropped it on the chair.

Something inside him seemed to snap at that, some last vestige of control finally giving way as he tore off his clothes and reached for her, drawing her up against his hot, naked and very willing body.

Hot. So hot. Hot and firm and taut with need, humming with that electric charge that seemed to fill them both. His hands ran over her back and stopped at her bra strap.

'You've got too much on,' he growled, and dealt with it, unclipping her bra, sliding down her jeans, hooking her underwear on the way so she ended up as naked as him, steadying herself with a hand on his head as he crouched down and peeled her jeans off one foot, then the other.

He worked his way slowly back up her body,

scattering kisses all over the place, turning her knees to jelly as he paused here and there for a little extra attention until they buckled and she sat down abruptly on the edge of the bed.

He tipped her back, rolled her over into the middle of the bed and followed her down onto the rumpled bedclothes, pulling her into his arms so they lay together face to face, toe to toe, heart to heart.

She could feel the thud of his heart against her ribs, the jut of his erection against the bowl of her pelvis, the rasp of his hair against her legs. Eyes locked on hers, he ran his hands slowly down her back and eased her closer, threading a leg between hers, a hand following it with unerring accuracy.

Too much. Too intense, too…

She closed her eyes, focusing on his hand, his body, the nudge of his erection as she rocked against his touch.

Her hands were exploring him, too, tracing the taut lines of his muscles, the jut of his hipbone, the texture of his skin, coarse here with hair, then silky smooth there, burning hot and humming with tension.

He shifted, bringing a hand up to her breasts, rolling her nipple between thumb and forefinger as his mouth laid a line of hot, moist kisses across her collarbones, up her throat, behind her ear.

She ran a hand up his back to cradle his head, threading her fingers through soft tousled hair as his lips found hers in a kiss that spiralled instantly out of control.

He wrenched away, breath hot against her face.

'Two seconds,' he muttered, and rolled away, groping on the bedside chest for that elusive foil packet. She heard him swear softly, then the tiny sound of tearing foil, and he was back, nudging her legs apart for him.

She was ready—so ready, but as her body welcomed his it took her breath away. His too. She heard his breath hiss out, and she gasped and clung to him as his hand found her again, his touch sure and deft. She felt the tension building in him, then a rising tide inside her as he thrust deeper, deeper and took her over the edge.

She bit his shoulder to stifle the scream, felt him stiffen, heard the deep, guttural groan of his climax as he shuddered in her arms, and then he dropped his head against hers, his breathing ragged, his heart hammering against her ribs as they came slowly back down to earth.

In more ways than one.

As their hearts slowed and the passion cooled on their skin, common sense resurrected itself.

What had she done?

He was a consultant in her department, for heaven's sake! And it was his first day, she knew nothing about him, he knew nothing about her—she must have been mad! And work was going to be so, so awkward...

He'd rolled away, and he was sitting up now on the edge of the bed, looking at her over his shoulder. 'Hey. It's OK,' he murmured. He reached out a hand and touched her cheek lightly, and then stood up and walked into the bathroom, closing the door behind him and leaving her there sprawled naked and sated on the mess that was her bed.

What had she done?

He closed the bathroom door behind him and caught his reflection in the mirror over the basin. There were toothmarks in his shoulder, and he couldn't meet his own eyes.

What had he done?

She was a midwife, and he was going to have to work with her over and over again, and he'd slept—no, scratch that, he'd had hot, hot sex with her. On his first day, for heaven's sake! He knew nothing about her, she knew nothing about him—not that there was a lot to know, apart from the fact that he'd used her to blank out the memories...

Don't think about it.

He pulled himself together and dealt with the condom—and stopped, horror washing over him. It was torn. Only a slight tear, but enough to have consequences.

As if it weren't already bad enough...

He washed his hands and went back out into her bedroom. She'd straightened out the bed and she was sitting up against the pillows, messy hair tumbling over her shoulders, the duvet hauled up around her like a force field, eyes wary as she looked at him.

He reached for his shorts. 'We need to talk,' he said bluntly, starting to pull on his clothes.

'Do we?'

'Yes. You need emergency contraception. The condom tore.'

Her gaze was steady, but there was something odd about it, about the way she held his eyes. Almost defiant.

'It's all right. You can't get me pregnant, if that's what you're worried about.'

He'd heard that before, and he searched her eyes for more clues. 'Are you sure?'

'As sure as I can be, and I haven't got any STIs you need to worry about either. I had all the tests in the world four years ago after my ex confessed he was having an affair, just to be on the safe side, and I haven't done this since, so—yeah. You're safe. I can't get pregnant, and I can't give you anything nasty. Your turn.'

He felt the tension leak out of him like air out of a punctured balloon. Or a ripped condom…

He shook his head. 'You won't get anything from me. I'm fanatical about it.'

'No other ruptured condoms or intimate disasters in your history?'

He could have laughed, but it wasn't funny. 'No ruptured condoms.' Just a catalogue of failures leading to the ultimate disaster…

Her shoulders dropped a fraction. 'Well, that's all right then. We're both off the hook. You can relax.'

Hardly, not while she was sitting there warm and rumpled and sexy as hell, her hair a tumbling waterfall of gold that made his fingers itch to touch it. He held her eyes for a moment longer, then nodded. 'OK. I need to go,' he said, and she looked away.

'Yes, you probably do. I've got an early start and I don't…'

He had no idea what she didn't, but he needed to fill the void in this conversation, say the words that still remained unsaid.

'Georgia, it's OK. This doesn't need to make life difficult. We're both adults. We can deal with this, but not now. I need to get back to the hospital and check on Susie and the baby.'

'Really? You could ring.'

'I could, but I'd rather go in. The registrar's overstretched, the F2 doesn't know one end of a baby from the other yet and I'd rather trust my own judgement.'

He reached for his trousers and pulled them on, tucked his shirt in and looked back at her.

'Are you in tomorrow?'

She nodded. 'Yes. I'm on at seven.'

'OK. I'll see you there. Maybe we can catch a coffee if there's time.'

He heard a little huff of laughter.

'In your wildest dreams. But yes, that would be good.'

She looked up again, and in her eyes there was understanding and maybe a tinge of regret. In a moment of impulse he leant in and touched his lips to her, then straightened up.

'Thank you.'

She raised an eyebrow. 'What for? Specifically?'

He felt his smile. Was it as crooked as it felt? Probably. 'Everything. Acting quickly with Susie, being there in Theatre, feeding me before I fell over—and this…this, whatever it was.'

She smiled back as crookedly as him, and shook her head slowly. 'I'll see you tomorrow.'

He nodded, picked up his keys, phone and wallet from her bedside chest, ran downstairs and let himself out.

And then stood there, his brain a mess, utterly disorientated. He had no idea where he was, where the hospital was, and how to find his way back there. With a sharp sigh he pulled out his phone, clicked on the map and followed it.

She slept like a log, to her surprise.

She hadn't thought she would, not after what they'd done, but clearly she wasn't as troubled by it as she probably should have been. Either that or it was the flood of endorphins he'd released in her.

She rolled out of bed, stretched luxuriously and headed for the shower, and half an hour later she walked onto the ward to find him standing at the central desk talking to Ben Walker, of all people. Clinical lead, highly perceptive human and husband of one of her friends.

Great, she thought, and braced herself for the inevitable awkwardness.

'Morning, Georgie. Have you met Dan?' Ben greeted her with his usual wide smile, and Dan looked round and gave a tiny nod of recognition. He looked as awkward as she felt, and every bit as appealing as he had last night.

She plastered a smile on her face and tried to ignore the hitch in her pulse. 'Yes, I have. Morning. So how's today shaping up so far, Ben? Chaos already?'

'I don't know. Probably, but Jan was looking out for you,' he told her, so she went to find her, glad of an excuse to get away because it was even more awkward than she'd imagined it was going to be, and she had no idea what to say to Dan. Easier to ignore it—and him.

She spotted Jan halfway down the corridor, just as her phone started ringing in her pocket. Livvy. She'd call her in a minute. 'Hi, Jan. I gather you want me.'

'Yes, Livvy Hunter came in a few minutes ago in established labour. I think she'd like you to deliver her, if you're happy to do that.'

Which explained the call. She felt a little bubble of excitement and beamed at Jan. 'I'd absolutely love to. Has anyone started with her?'

'No, not yet. I've just got her notes up from the clinic. Her husband's with her. She's in Room Four, settling in.'

Susie's room. Hopefully it wouldn't be a bad omen. She popped her head round the door.

'Hi, Livvy, hi, Matt. How are you doing?'

Matt and Livvy both gave her a relieved smile.

'Oh, Georgie, I'm so glad you're here,' Livvy said. 'I just tried to ring you. It's happening so fast. Can you be with me?'

'Yes, I've already cleared it with Jan. Give me two seconds to change. I've literally just walked onto the ward.'

'Don't be long. I've got contractions every two minutes.'

'I won't be. Just keep breathing.'

She went into the locker room as Dan was leaving.

'Are we OK?' he asked, his voice low and all chocolatey again, and her heart did a silly backflip.

'Yes, of course,' she said, not at all sure and trying hard to ignore her heart and meet his eyes. 'Busy. One of our ED doctors is in labour, so that's my day taken care of.'

'You never know, it might be quick.'

She rolled her eyes. 'Now don't jinx it, you should know better. Jan did that to me with Susie. How is she, by the way? Did you see her last night?'

'Yes, and again this morning. She's doing

OK, and the baby's fine, he's all good, feeding well, no apparent neurological deficit. She asked me to thank you. You should pop up and see them when you get a minute. And shout if you need me.'

'I will.'

She didn't need him.

Well, not for Livvy. For herself? That was a totally different question, and not one for now, when her friend was in labour and moving very fast, unless she was mistaken.

Livvy was lying on her side facing Matt and getting a bit stroppy with him by the time Georgie went back in. Matt was trying not to smile and doing his level best to be supportive, but Livvy wasn't having any of it.

'You're doing really well,' he murmured, and she glared at him.

'No thanks to you. It's entirely your fault I'm in this mess, and I don't want to do it any more. I'm going home. I'm too tired to do this now. I didn't sleep all night, and I just— aahh....'

Georgie went over to her and laid a hand on her side. 'It's OK, Livvy, breathe through it, nice gentle little pants—'

'I am breathing!' she snarled, and Georgie met Matt's eyes and smiled.

'Transition,' she mouthed, and he grinned. 'Looks like it.'

'Will you two stop whispering about me and shut up?' Livvy yelled, and Georgie reached over and pressed the call button to summon another midwife for the imminent delivery. A few seconds later she heard a soft knock and the click of the door opening.

She looked over her shoulder and found Dan there, one eyebrow slightly raised. 'Anything I can do?' he murmured.

'Not unless you're a midwife.'

He smiled slightly. 'Sorry, no, but they're all tied up according to Jan. Will I do instead?'

'I don't know. Looks like we'll find out,' she said with a wry smile. 'Livvy, Matt, this is Dan Blake, our new consultant. He obviously doesn't have enough to do today, so are you OK if he hangs out with us and plays midwife?'

'He can hang out wherever he likes so long as one of you useless people gets this baby out!' Livvy snapped over her shoulder, and then she reached out and grabbed Matt's hand and Georgie saw him wince.

She turned to Dan and threw him an apron. 'Here you go. You can see how it happens when you're not needed.'

He chuckled softly, snapped on a pair of

gloves and did as he was told, which was more than Livvy did when she examined her.

'Stop doing that, I need to push!'

'Not yet, there's a tiny lip of cervix left, Livvy, just keep panting for a moment, it's nearly gone—'

'I don't want to pant, I want to push and it's my baby so I'm going to push!' she growled, and then she grabbed Matt and pulled herself up onto her knees and flung her arms around his neck.

'Ow-ow-ow, it hurts,' she wailed, and he rubbed her back and murmured soft encouraging words in her ear as Georgie crouched down and checked the baby's progress again.

'Steady, Livvy, you're nearly there, the baby's crowning now. Soft pants, no pushing—that's lovely, Livvy, that's brilliant, nice and gentle—and here we go,' she added, catching the baby and passing it through Livvy's legs as she sank down onto the bed.

'It's a girl. Time of birth: seven-thirty-eight a.m.,' she said to Dan, and he nodded and handed her a warmed towel to wrap the baby in as Matt lowered Livvy gently back against the pillows.

'Hello, my precious one,' Livvy crooned softly, and Georgie lifted the baby and laid her on her waiting mother's bare skin, tucking the towel in round her. She let out a wail, then another one, her skin pinking up instantly, and Matt bent over and pressed his lips to Livvy's hair, his eyes squeezed tight shut.

'Well done, my love. You were amazing.'

She looked up at him, her eyes sparkling with tears, and smiled. 'I don't think I was. Was I horrible?'

'No, of course you weren't horrible, you were brilliant,' he murmured, and Georgie turned away, partly to give them both a moment and partly to hide her smile.

'Apgar ten at one minute,' she said, and Dan nodded again.

He'd already done it, she could see it on the screen as he filled in the notes by hand and onto the computer. He'd also drawn up the oxytocin.

'Thanks. You're actually quite useful to have around,' she said with a wry smile, and he raised an eyebrow and his eyes crinkled at the sides.

'Likewise. Nice delivery, by the way. You're good.'

'Just doing my job,' she said, but she turned back to Livvy and Matt with a warm glow inside, still smiling at his words.

'Oh, she's beautiful. Congratulations. Does she have a name?'

'Esme.' Livvy smiled and looked up at Matt. 'Esme Juliet.'

For Matt's first wife, Amber and Charlie's mother. 'Oh, that's lovely,' she said softly, swallowing a lump, and she wrote the baby's name on her label, slipped it into the tiny name band and clipped it around the baby's ankle.

'Well done, Livvy, I'm so happy for you both,' she murmured, and Livvy gave her a wobbly smile and reached out an arm and hugged her.

'Thank you so much. That was amazing. I can't believe we've actually got a baby…'

She started to cry, and Matt wrapped his arm around her and hugged her against his chest. They'd been through so much between them, both separately and together, and to reach this point was little short of a miracle, so it was small wonder they were both in tears.

She'd be in tears under the circumstances. Not that it was ever going to happen, not to her…

'You OK?'

Dan's voice was the merest murmur, and she blinked hard and nodded. 'Of course. Why wouldn't I be?' she murmured back, and busied herself with the notes, glad of something to do.

She heard Dan's phone buzz next to the computer, and he met her eyes.

'Are you OK if I go? Someone needs a ventouse by the sound of it. I shouldn't be long.'

'I should think so. You could bring us all back a cup of tea when you've done it. We'll be ready by then.'

His mouth quirked and he rolled his eyes, waved his fingers at Matt and Livvy and left, and Georgie turned her attention back to Livvy and the baby.

'OK, little Esme, let's have a look at you, shall we?'

She did a rapid check to make sure all was present and correct, clipped and cut the cord and put a nappy on the by then furious baby and handed her back to her mother. She instantly started rooting, her little rosebud mouth nuzzling at her mother, and Matt lifted a hand and stroked her tiny head.

'She's hungry,' he murmured, and Georgie nodded.

'She is. Livvy, have you had any more thoughts about breastfeeding?' she asked gently, deeply conscious of her breast cancer history and her concerns about whether she'd be able to manage it, and Livvy nodded.

'I want to try,' she said. 'This cancer's taken enough from me, but if I can't, I don't care because we've got our baby and that's all that really matters.'

'Well, let's see what we can do,' she said, and calmly and quietly positioned the baby and helped her latch on. It took two attempts, but then she was there, suckling hard, and Livvy's eyes filled with tears.

'Wow. Oh, clever baby!' she whispered, and she took the baby's tiny hand in hers and held it as she fed.

Her tiny rosebud lips went slack after a few moments, but Livvy held her there, staring down at her with such love that Georgie had to turn away.

She went back to the paperwork, leaving the three of them bonding, but she couldn't see. She blinked hard and tried to blot out her thoughts, but it was hard when all she could think about was the futility of that torn condom, and the babies she'd never have.

Maybe she needed a man like Matt, a man who already had children, but that would do nothing to quell the biological ache inside her every time a woman gave birth.

Maybe she didn't need a man at all. Maybe she needed a different job so she wasn't confronted by her own sorrow on a daily basis.

But for now she had this one, and she owed it to Livvy to do it properly. The baby was still suckling in between little moments of sleep, and judging by the look on Livvy's face everything was right in her world. Not so Matt's, she thought, catching a glimpse of another emotion on his face, and her heart ached for him.

'Are you OK if I go and grab a coffee, Olivia?' he murmured, and Livvy smiled up at him and stroked his cheek gently.

'Sure, darling. We're not going anywhere.'

'I won't be long.'

Georgie watched him go, then finished what she was doing and turned to Livvy.

'I just need to pop out for a minute. Press the call button if you need me, I won't be far away,' she said, and followed Matt out. She was almost sure he wasn't going for a coffee, so she headed off the ward and found him just outside, near the lifts.

He was standing by the window, staring out blindly across the car park, and she walked over to him and laid a hand on his arm.

'Are you OK?' she asked softly, and he swallowed hard and nodded.

'Yeah. Just—memories.'

Of the birth of his first two children, to the mother they'd lost far, far too young. 'Take your time,' she said gently. 'I'll be with her. She won't be alone.'

He nodded again, turning this time to hug

her, his voice gruff. 'Thank you, Georgie. You've been a star.'

'Just doing my job, Matt.'

'Yeah, right,' he said, his grin a little crooked. 'I might go and grab that coffee now.'

'Good idea. You can always bring it back with you.'

'I might do that.'

She left him there with his thoughts, and headed back to Livvy. 'Everything OK?'

Livvy nodded. 'I've got the odd contraction, and I sort of feel I want to push?'

'That's good. Let's have a look. I expect your placenta's detached now.'

She'd just lifted it into a bowl and was tidying up when there was a tap on the door and Dan came back in.

'Are we ready for tea?'

She smiled at him. 'I was joking, but yes, that would be lovely. Dan's gone to get a coffee, but I'm always ready. Livvy?'

'Oh, yes, please. White, no sugar.'

'Ditto... Or I can make it and you can check the placenta?'

He grinned. 'You'd trust me?'

'With the placenta, yes. With the tea? Not so much.'

His lips twitched. 'D'you know what? You've

got gloves on, I haven't. You do the placenta. I'll make the tea.'

The door clicked shut behind him, and Livvy gave her a curious look.

'You're getting on well. Do you know each other?'

Well, that was a loaded question, with a not so obvious answer. 'No, not at all, I only met him yesterday,' she said, trying to sound casual, 'but we worked together on a case. He seems OK. Good team player, very easy-going.'

'Hmm,' Livvy said, not sounding convinced, and Georgie ignored her and busied herself with the placenta.

'How are you feeling?' she asked, and Livvy gave a weary laugh.

'Happy? A bit sore? And very, very tired! I don't think I slept all night.'

'I'm sure. You've done really well. I'll take Esme off you in a minute so you can relax. I need to weigh and measure her, then clean her up a little and get her dressed, and Dan should be back soon with the tea.'

He was. She'd hardly said the words when he came back in, juggling three mugs and a plate of biscuits on a tray.

'Ooh, you found some biscuits.'

He looked a little guilty. 'Actually Jan found them.'

'So who made the tea? And don't give me the side eye, I'm only teasing.'

'You're rude. FYI, I made the tea.'

Livvy laughed and held her hand out for a mug, and he set the tray down, scooped up the baby with practised hands and passed her a mug, then peered at the placenta over Georgie's shoulder.

'Is it OK? As I have a vested interest, in that it'll be me dealing with the fallout.'

'No fallout,' she told him, and stripping off her gloves, she picked up a mug and peered at it. 'Well, there's a miracle. A decent cup of tea.'

'I am housetrained,' he said, sounding indignant, but she didn't bother to reply because Matt came back in then, with a coffee in one hand and a paper bag that looked suspiciously like a cake in the other.

'Here you go. A little present for the star of the day,' he said with a smile and handed it to Livvy, then took the baby from Dan, kissed her and tucked her into the crook of his arm like the seasoned father he was.

Dan picked up his tea and came and stood beside Georgie, so close she could feel the heat of his body, smell the soap on his skin, feel the drift of his breath against her cheek.

'Do you need me?'

Another loaded question.

'No, you're fine. I'm sure there are a million other things you should be doing, but thank you for your help with this.'

'It's what I'm here for, but you're right, there's a mountain of stuff I should be doing.'

He congratulated Matt and Livvy again and left, and she felt the tension drain out of her, but underneath she could still feel something unsettling, a seething, bubbling sensation of unfinished business between them.

Her own stupid fault. She should have let him go when he suggested it instead of dragging him upstairs and creating havoc between them. She finished her tea, put the mug down and got on with her job.

CHAPTER THREE

'JAN, I NEED a break. Can I grab half an hour? It's after one and I haven't stopped for a second yet.'

She hesitated, then gave a brisk nod. 'OK— but just half an hour, Georgie. I can't spare you any longer.'

'Thank you, you're a star.'

She headed off the ward, running downstairs before Jan had time to change her mind, and at the bottom of the stairs she bumped into Dan. Literally.

He caught her arms before she slammed into him, and grinned. 'Whoa! What are you running away from?'

She took a hasty step back, away from all that warm charisma. 'To, not from. I'm going for lunch.'

'Don't bother. The canteen's ramming.'

'Always is. I'm going to the Park Café. That's normally OK.'

'Really?' His eyes lit up. 'Mind if I join you?'

Did she mind? No. Was it a good idea? Big fat no this time, but she couldn't be that churlish.

'Sure,' she said, and let them out of the back doors into the beautiful park that surrounded the hospital, walking briskly over the grass to the Park Café near the back of the ED.

As she'd predicted it wasn't too busy, and she grabbed a banana and a muffin, ordered a cappuccino and plonked them on the tray next to his sandwich, black espresso and bottle of water.

'I'm getting this,' he said firmly as they reached the till, and she laughed.

'Go for it, but you still owe me dinner,' she joked, and then could have bitten her tongue off.

Why say that? Why poke the sleeping tiger?

But he just rolled his eyes, picked up the tray and raised a questioning eyebrow, and she led him outside.

'I need the shade, there's a bench over there,' she said, heading for a tree, and he followed her with the tray, swept a few crumbs off the seat and put the tray down between them.

'Good sandwich,' he mumbled round a mouthful, and she picked up her blueberry muffin and nodded.

'They are. I didn't want anything that healthy today, I just need quick calories. I haven't stopped since you left. Thanks again for your help with Livvy, by the way. You'll make a good midwife if you ever need a career change.'

He chuckled. 'You're welcome. It's nice to see it all happen as it should.' Then his smile faded and he tilted his head on one side and gave her a thoughtful look. 'So what's the story with those two? The atmosphere was loaded, and Matt looked—I don't know. A bit overwhelmed. Haunted, maybe, if that doesn't sound a bit far-fetched.'

She nodded. 'No, you're spot on, I think he was. He lost his first wife when his children were tiny, and Livvy's had breast cancer.'

His eyes widened and he went still. 'Whoa. Did he know that before they got married?'

'Yes. Oh, yes.'

He looked down, his face suddenly sombre. 'Wow. That must have taken some courage, marrying someone else who might die when you've already lost your wife.'

'But he loves her, and she'd had the all-clear, but one thing I know. Neither of them will ever take anything for granted.'

'No, I don't suppose they would.' He shook his head slowly. 'That's a heck of a journey to this point.'

'It is, but love can give you the strength to do all sorts of things. Anyway, this baby's really quite a big deal, and I'm so happy for them that they've been able to do it.'

He was studying her oddly. 'Are you?' he asked, and his words caught her by surprise.

'Well, of course I am. Why wouldn't I be?'

He shrugged. 'I don't know, you tell me. I mean, I'm sure you are, you're that sort of person, but for a second or two in there you didn't quite look it.'

She dragged her eyes away from his and drained her coffee. 'I don't know what you think you saw, but I'm fine.'

His voice was soft. 'Are you? Are you really?'

That again. She was opening her mouth to say something—she hadn't quite decided what—when he crumpled his cup and stood up.

'Look, I have to go, I've got an antenatal clinic in a minute, but I think we need to talk,' he said quietly.

'About?'

'Last night. It raised some—issues.'

'Issues?' she said, puzzled. She thought—

'Issues,' he said firmly. 'We need a conversation, but not here, we don't have time and it's too public for what I have to say, and anyway, as you quite rightly pointed out, I owe you dinner. Mine tonight, seven-thirty?'

'That was a joke.'

'Not to me. Please?'

She hesitated, not convinced it was in the slightest bit wise because last night was all she'd been able to think about ever since, and rehashing it seemed like the worst idea in the world. And anyway, she thought they'd already dealt with it.

'No strings, Georgia, I just want to talk to you,' he said, as if he could read her mind, and so she gave him her phone number so he could text her his address, threw her coffee cup in the bin and headed back to the ward, wondering what on earth she'd let herself in for.

Trouble, without a doubt, and she wasn't looking forward to it one little bit.

Livvy and her tiny daughter were discharged at three, and she escorted them to the door, watched as Matt clipped the baby seat with its precious cargo into the car, and kissed Livvy goodbye.

'I'll pop round and see you tomorrow,' she promised, and Livvy nodded.

'That'll be lovely. You can hold my hand and tell me it'll be OK.'

She laughed at that and hugged her. 'Of

course it'll be OK. You're a natural. Go on, go home to Amber and Charlie and let them meet their baby sister.'

She waved them off and swallowed the lump in her throat. Was she the only person in the world who wasn't pregnant, smothered in tiny people or planning their wedding?

Laura and Tom were next in line of her friends, with a baby due in January. Another one she'd been asked to deliver, courtesy of their mutual friendship with Livvy Hunter. She didn't really know Laura, she'd only met her a few times, but like Livvy she seemed blissfully happy.

And Susie, too. She popped in briefly to see her on the way back to the ward, and found her sitting out in a chair with her little boy in her arms and her clearly besotted partner Rob at her side. They were the picture of happiness, and she was truly glad for them that it had turned out all right in the end, but still, under it all was that gnawing ache, the longing for what she'd lost when Mark had walked away. Although to be fair she'd never had it, but he'd just rubbed it in in the cruellest way.

You don't need a man in your life.

She didn't. She really didn't—especially not one like Mark, who hadn't even had the grace to tell her he wanted to move on until his girlfriend was pregnant. Or like Dan, come to that, considering she had to work with him, because the almost visceral tug between them was trashing her peace of mind.

Last night was *such* a bad idea. And now he wanted to talk about it?

She said goodbye and hurried back to the ward, for once in her life hoping it would be really busy, and she got her wish. Everyone in a fifty-mile radius seemed to be in labour, and she was straight back into the fray, which was just as well as it saved her from wallowing in self-pity.

Either that, or trying to work out what on earth Dan wanted to talk about, because she thought they'd dealt with the condom issue, and she couldn't think what else there was to talk about—apart from the fact that falling into bed with a colleague wasn't the smartest trick they could have pulled.

Still, four hours to go and she'd find out, and until then she was in charge of ensuring that other people got their miracle safe and sound. The miracle she'd never have.

She *really* needed a different job…

She was late leaving, of course. Only an hour, for a change, but she'd run home, had the quickest shower on record and pulled on the first thing she'd found that was cool enough, grabbed a jumper on the way out and left.

She turned into Brooke Avenue at seven-thirty-four and walked briskly along it, checking the numbers. Thirty-eight...forty—ah, here it was. Forty-two.

She stopped and stared at it curiously. It was Tom and Laura's house—or at least, Tom's old house. She'd only seen it once when she, Livvy and Laura had been out for a walk with Laura's dog, Millie, but she was sure it was the one.

It must have had a bit of a makeover in the last few weeks, though. The peeling woodwork had all been painted a soft grey-green, the rendered walls not quite white, and it was a charming, welcoming little cottage now instead of a slightly tired one.

She rang the bell, and after a second she heard footsteps running down the stairs and the door opened to reveal Dan barefoot, towel-dried hair on end, in the act of tugging on a T-shirt over his damp and really rather beautiful chest.

Don't bother on my account, she thought, and then spotted the bite mark on his shoulder before it disappeared under the T. Really? Had she done that to him last night? Heat washed through her at the thought, and she cut herself off before she lost the plot. She was there because he wanted to talk, not…

'Hi. Sorry, I got held up as I was leaving so I've only been home ten minutes. Come in.'

'I've only just finished, too,' she said, hoping her voice didn't sound as ridiculously breathless as she felt. 'It's been manic there today.'

'Tell me about it, but it doesn't matter, we're both here now and the food won't take long. Come on through, I'll get you a drink and you can talk to me while I cook.'

'What are we having?' she asked, to fill the void as much as anything. Not that she wasn't hungry—

'Mushroom stroganoff with wild rice, if that's OK, and I thought steamed veg. Green beans, tenderstem broccoli, sugar snap peas, julienne carrots—whatever you fancy, really. Is that all right?'

She gave a surprised laugh. 'Wow, that's a lot of options. Have you just been shopping or something?'

He chuckled at that and raked a hand through his hair. 'No. I had a delivery the day before yesterday, and I was going to cook last night except you got there first.'

And look how that went…

'It sounds delicious,' she said, cutting off

her thoughts yet again before they strayed into dangerous territory, and followed him through to the kitchen.

'Make yourself at home,' he said, and delved into the fridge, so she settled herself in a chair and plucked a grape off the bunch in the fruit bowl to tide her over.

'So how come you're renting Tom Stryker's house?' she asked curiously.

'You know them?'

'Yes—well, I know Laura through Livvy, and I've seen Tom in the ED when I've been called down there. She's pregnant, too, due in January.'

'Another one?'

'Oh, it's rife.' Rife amongst her peer group, anyway. She couldn't get away from it, and every birth, although it brought her joy for her friends, just twisted the knife a little more. 'So how come you're here? I didn't know it was ready to rent, they've been working on it.'

He shut the door of the fridge and put a pile of things down on the worktop. 'Ben Walker told me about it. He asked if I had anything in mind when I was offered the job, and this came up a few weeks ago, and I love it. It's got a gorgeous garden, and it'll give me time to sell my house in Bristol and look for something more permanent. What would you like to drink? I've got wine, red or white, or pome-granate and elderflower cordial, beer with or without, tea, coffee?'

She debated the cordial for a second, then gave in and shrugged. 'D'you know what? I'm not working tomorrow, I have the miracle of a day off, so I might go for a white wine.'

Which was probably a mistake, because her guard had been well and truly down when she was stone cold sober...

Not an issue. For now at least he was busy chopping, slicing, frying, stirring, warming plates, so she stayed put and sipped her wine, raided the grapes and watched him, and within twenty minutes they were sitting down at a table in the garden with a steaming plate full of loveliness.

'Gosh, that smells good,' she said, and dived in. 'Mmm. Super-tasty,' she mumbled, and he gave a wry laugh.

'You really didn't think it would be, did you?'

She looked up and met his eyes, and they were oddly humourless despite the laugh. 'I didn't know what to expect,' she said, not only about the food but about him, what he wanted to talk about, what he wanted with her. If any-thing...

And then she couldn't wait any longer. 'You

said you wanted to talk,' she said, and he put his fork down with exaggerated care.

'Yes. Yes, I did.' His eyes flicked up and locked on hers, oddly penetrating. 'You said last night I couldn't get you pregnant. You sounded very sure.'

She dropped her eyes back to her food, suddenly flavourless and unappealing. 'I am sure.'

'Why?'

'I just am.'

He gave a short sigh. 'Georgia, I need to know,' he said quietly, but with a thread of steel. 'If you get pregnant, it's on me, and I really don't want that to happen.'

'It can't happen,' she said, dropping her fork and meeting his eyes with difficulty. 'I can't get pregnant. My ex and I spent four years trying, and I mean *really* trying, and nothing happened, so I suggested having some investigations, and then he told me he was having an affair and his girlfriend was pregnant.'

His jaw dropped. 'While you were still trying?'

She nodded. 'Oh, yeah. Well, I was. He was just having his cake and eating it, only he preferred her cake. He said all we ever did was try and make a baby, but with her sex was fun, only apparently it came with a side order of an unplanned pregnancy.'

He frowned. 'It couldn't have been some-one else's?'

'No. Oh, no, it was definitely his. She only lived round the corner, and he moved in with her after I kicked him out, and I bumped into them all the time. The child was the spitting image of him. That was when I moved here. I didn't need my nose rubbed in it every time I went out of my front door.'

'Hell, Georgie, that's...' He blew out his breath slowly, shaking his head. 'I'm sorry. Last night I thought you meant you were using some method of contraception, but after I saw you with Livvy Hunter...'

'Livvy?'

He shrugged. 'You had a look about you that I've seen before. A heartbreaking sort of "why not me?" look.'

She swallowed and looked down at her food. Was it really so obvious?

He reached out and laid his hand over hers. 'I'm sorry, I didn't mean to probe or upset you. I've got a few of my own hot buttons, but I sensed there was something about Livvy that touched one of yours, and it seems I wasn't wrong.'

No, he wasn't, of course, and every birth had an element of 'why not me', but it was an odd remark, something about the way he'd phrased

it. Not the bit about her, but the bit about him
and his hot buttons.

She studied his face, looking for a clue, and
she found one there in the shadows, some hint
of grief, perhaps, that she hadn't expected—
and doing Susie's section he'd been weird, in a
way, almost as if his emotions were shut down.
And he'd talked about a sore point.

His hot button?

'What happened to you, Dan?' she asked
gently, and he pushed his plate away and met
her eyes

'I can't eat this now. Let's go down the garden.'

He got to his feet, and she followed him
past the late-blooming roses, the blaze of blue
from the agapanthus, the brilliant white of the
Japanese anemones mingling with them at the
back of the border behind the delicate froth
of baby's breath and the mounds of soft pink
geraniums. There was a bench at the far end
under a tree, surrounded by the sweet scent of
nicotiana and night-scented stocks, and they
sat down on it, tilted their faces to the evening
sun and she waited.

And waited.

Then finally, when she was about to prompt
him, he spoke, his voice soft and a little raw.

'I was with someone at uni. We'd been together for a few months, and we got careless. She was on the pill, but she'd had a bug, and we didn't even think about it, and she ended up pregnant. It couldn't have been at a worse time. We were about to start our first jobs, and although we were both in London we weren't in the same hospital, and living together would have meant a long commute. So I was in hospital accommodation on the other side of London, and we were hardly seeing each other and our relationship suffered. When she told me she was pregnant we even talked about getting married, but she didn't think it was a good enough reason and I agreed, really. I fully intended to have a relationship with my child, and I was there for all the scans and really looking forward to meeting the baby, and we were both OK with that, but not with us. We weren't really getting on by then and it wouldn't have lasted, but at least if we'd been together still I might have been there with her when it happened. I should have been there, and she should never have got pregnant, and that was my fault and I'll blame myself for ever.

'Anyway, it made no difference in the end. She was diagnosed with a placenta previa at her anomaly scan, which was pretty worrying, and she was booked for an elective section at thirty-eight weeks, with constant monitoring. And it was all going well, and then one day, when she was thirty-four weeks, I missed a call from her, and I didn't pick up her voice-mail for half an hour. She'd started to bleed, and she'd called an ambulance. She sounded terrified, and I hadn't picked up because it was on silent and I'd missed her call.'

Georgie closed her eyes, not sure she wanted to hear what she knew was coming.

'I got there just as they were taking her to Theatre. She was still conscious, barely, and she made me promise I'd look after the baby if anything happened to her. I told her I would, and I told her she'd be fine, but she wasn't. I walked up and down outside Theatre, holding my breath for a little cry, but there was nothing, and then after an age the doors opened and the surgeon came out and told me she'd bled out. Her cervix had opened, and her placenta had pulled away and torn a major uterine vessel, and there was nothing they could do to save either of them.'

Horror washed over her at his quiet words, and her eyes welled. How on earth had he dealt with that?

'Oh, Dan, I'm so sorry. That's just heart-breaking.'

'It was. It tore me apart and it took a long

time to put myself back together. And then Susie on my first day—that was just classic timing.'

'That must have been so hard for you.'

He gave her a sad, twisted little smile. 'It was, but it's why I went into obstetrics. I couldn't save them, but maybe I could save someone else. Someone like Susie, and her baby. That's why I was so determined to save both of them, because if I didn't I knew exactly what Rob would be going through. When that baby cried…'

'Yes. I think we all nearly cried with it.' She reached out and took his hand, folding it in hers. 'Did you see your baby?' she asked gently, and she felt his hand tighten.

He nodded. 'A midwife took me into a quiet room and gave her to me to hold. She was beautiful, Georgie, absolutely perfect, and there was no need for her to have died. If we'd been living together, if we'd got married, if I'd answered my phone that day, maybe I could have saved her. Saved both of them.'

'Could you? Could you honestly? It doesn't sound like it.'

'I don't know. They said not. It had been too quick, too catastrophic. The midwife was lovely to me, really kind, and I'll be forever grateful to her for that. She'd taken little footprints, and she'd washed and dressed her and wrapped her in a blanket, and she put her in my arms and sat with me, and then she held me when I cried. You know how it goes, I'm sure you've done it.'

Georgie felt her eyes fill with tears. 'Yes, I have.' She'd done the same thing for bereaved parents more times than she wanted to think about, and it never got easier. And he'd lost his partner as well, although they weren't together.

What an awful, dreadful tragedy for all of them.

'Holly's parents took charge after that,' he went on, 'and arranged the funeral at their home, and they shut me out. I think they blamed me for getting her pregnant, and to be fair I blamed myself, for that and for not being there for her when she needed me. I still do. I always will, even though she'd pushed me away. So I wouldn't have gone to the funeral anyway, but it hurt that I wasn't there to hold Holly's hand when it mattered most, and it really, really hurt that our baby died. I didn't know what love was until I held my daughter in my arms, Georgie, and I'll always be gutted that she'll never know how much I wanted her...'

'Oh, Dan, I'm so sorry.'

'Yeah.' His voice cracked, and he cleared

his throat, paused for a moment, then went on, 'So, anyway, when I saw Susie, with no antenatal records on her and a bleeding placenta previa...'

'...it hit all your hot buttons.'

'Pretty much. Did it show?'

'A bit. You were very on it, and I thought, good, someone decisive, someone who knows what they're doing, but there was just something about you, an intensity, some undercurrent of something that I didn't quite understand.'

'Like you with Livvy.'

'Maybe. I understand a little of how they felt when they weren't sure if she'd be able to have a baby, so of course I'm pleased for them, but yes, I felt it. I always feel it, with every delivery. Don't get me wrong, I love my job, and I couldn't bear to give it up, but every baby I deliver, a little bit more inside me dies. I didn't realise it showed, though.'

'Likewise.'

She laughed, but it was a sad little effort. 'We wouldn't be any good at poker, would we?'

He gave her a wry, sad little smile. 'Probably not. Anyway, I was a bit raw after all the drama with Susie, and you were there, and you were kind to me, and I didn't want to talk about it, but there was all that warmth and kindness in your eyes, and I just wanted to hold you and let it soak into me and blot out all the memories.'

He lifted her hand and pressed it to his lips, then laid it down and met her eyes. 'I used you, and I'm sorry. It won't happen again.'

She shook her head, lifted her hand and cradled his cheek against her palm. 'I can't let you take responsibility for that. I said you didn't have to go. You didn't use me. OK, you weren't up front about your personal history, but we'd barely met, and things like that—they make us vulnerable, and I think we have to hold onto them a little longer, until we feel safe enough to share them. Like I didn't tell you about my infertility.'

He nodded slowly, then searched her eyes. 'Does that mean you feel safe with me now?'

She smiled at him and dropped her hand. 'Yes. Yes, I do. Is it a good idea going there again? Probably not.'

'No. You're right, and I was coming to that. I—I really don't think we should go there again. I don't think it would be wise. I need to be able to concentrate on settling into my new job, and I'm not really in the market for a relationship, especially not one where we'll end up working together all the time. It's got too much potential to get really messy, but I can always use a friend.'

'Well, I'm here,' she said, and his mouth twisted into a sad little parody of a smile.

'Yes, I think you are. Thank you.' He gave a wry laugh. 'Given our histories, do you ever get the feeling we're in the wrong jobs?'

That made her laugh, too, because she'd had that very thought earlier, with Livvy. 'All the time, but what else would we do? We'd both miss it, you know that. At least this way we get to make a difference.' She tilted her head on one side and smiled at him. 'Do you know what? I'm hungry now. Shall we go and eat?'

His mouth tilted, this time into a proper smile. 'Good idea. I'll warm it up.'

He walked her home, but not until they'd talked more about their jobs, the people he'd be working with, the ethos of the department.

All nice and safe, one of them at each end of the sofa, sipping coffee and exchanging anecdotes.

Being friends.

Until they ran out of safe topics, and then all of a sudden the tension was back, that invisible tug that was so dangerous, so beguiling, so very much not a good idea. She got up to leave and he insisted on walking with her.

'I'll be fine,' she told him, but he shook his head.

'I've got enough on my conscience, I don't need you as well,' he said, and so she stopped arguing and let him do it.

Not that she could have stopped him. She might not know him well, but she knew him that well already, and it was oddly reassuring.

They reached her door, and he stopped, just out of reach, while she slipped her key into the lock and turned it.

She left the door open and turned back to him with a smile, but something in his eyes stopped her smile in its tracks. A lingering trace of grief, of emptiness, of loneliness and longing that echoed her own.

For an age he held her eyes, then looked down, hands rammed in his pockets as if to stop them reaching out to her.

'I need to go,' he said gruffly, and she was so, so close to telling him to stay, because if a man ever needed someone to hold him Dan did then, but he took a step back as if he knew what she was thinking, and threw her a wry smile. 'Have a good day off.'

'I will. And thank you for supper. It was delicious.'

'You're welcome. Goodnight, Georgia.'

And without waiting for a reply he turned on his heel and walked away, striding off into the night with his back ramrod straight.

She could have followed him, called out, run after him—but she didn't. Her shoulders dropped, the tension of the moment leaving her, replaced in the nick of time by common sense.

He was right. It was too complicated, with them working together and him carrying the burden of his grief and guilt still, after ten years. He didn't need her, and especially not now while he was settling into a new role in a new hospital.

And when he did need someone there for him, it would be someone who could give him children. Someone who could give him the family he so deserved. That wasn't her, and never would be, but in the meantime she could be his friend.

Even if it killed her...

She went inside and shut the door.

Had it cleared the air?

He wasn't sure. He hoped so, but there was

a niggle of regret that he hadn't taken her up on the invitation in her eyes.

Maybe he'd misread it, the light from her porch playing tricks with him. And even if he hadn't, it wasn't a good idea. Sleeping with a colleague that you had to work with all the time was never a good idea, and he really needed his mind clear to concentrate on settling into his new role.

Never mind the fact that once again he would have been using her to blot out the memories. Using her, after he'd promised it would never happen again.

He let himself in, closed the front door firmly behind him and set about eradicating all trace of her from the house. He loaded the dishwasher, tipped out the last dreg of wine from her glass, added it to the top rack and shut the door on it, then turned and spotted her jumper draped over the back of a dining chair.

She'd brought it in case it got chilly, but it hadn't, and she'd left it behind. He picked it up and buried his nose in it and breathed her in, then threw it down, cross with himself for giving in to the impulse.

It had only made it worse, brought back the memories of last night, the scent of her hair, the warmth of her body, the sound of her as she—

'Stop it! It's not appropriate, and anyway, you're broken, you're no use to her. Not going to happen.'

He turned on the cold tap, ran it for a moment, filled a glass with fresh water and took it up to bed. If all else failed, he could tip it over himself...

CHAPTER FOUR

SHE WENT TO see Livvy at eleven the next morning, armed with flowers, a present for the baby and a game for the older two, and found her resting in the shade on the swing seat at the end of the garden, her baby in her arms and a tender smile on her face.

'Olivia, look who's here,' Matt said, and she looked up and smiled.

'Georgie! Oh, they're beautiful. Thank you—and what are all these? You shouldn't have...'

'Rubbish.' She bent and kissed Livvy's cheek, and smiled down at the baby. 'Oh, she's so beautiful. Hello, little Esme.' She perched on the end of the bench and put all the presents down, and Matt rescued the flowers and took them inside, leaving them to talk. 'So, how's it going?' she asked. 'Are you managing to breastfeed her?'

Livvy nodded. 'Yes. I think it might be a

bit more difficult when my milk comes in because of the tug on the scar tissue, but, d'you know what? I've had worse, and it's worth it, and I'm sure I'll soon adjust.'

'You can always talk to a breastfeeding counsellor.'

'I know. My midwife came this morning and we talked about it. I'm so glad it was you who delivered me, though. I mean, she's lovely, but I just felt you understood us and our situation and we didn't need to explain anything. Matt said you were really kind to him when he was having a moment.'

She shrugged. 'I just tried to put myself in his shoes. It must be very bittersweet.'

'Yes, it is. But he's so thrilled with her, he's utterly besotted, and Amber and Charlie are just over the moon. Especially Amber. I think she views her baby sister as a real live doll she can help to look after, and she's so gentle with her.'

'I'm sure they'll have great fun.'

'I hope so. It might take a bit of getting used to, though. So what's in here?' she added, putting one hand in the baby gift bag and pulling out the contents. 'Oh, Georgie! Oh, it's so soft and squishy! Thank you!'

She snuggled the little grey rabbit up against her face, and sighed. 'It's lovely. Thank you so much.'

'You're welcome. And that's just a little game for the other two to play when they get bored with Esme,' she said with a smile.

Matt reappeared with ice-cold glasses of elderflower cordial beaded with moisture and a plate of biscuits made by the children, taking the presents back inside with him and leaving them alone, and Livvy took a sip of her drink and leant back and eyed Georgie thoughtfully. Too thoughtfully.

'What?' she asked round a mouthful of choc chip cookie.

'This Dan guy. I know I was a bit distracted yesterday, not to mention a total diva, sorry about that, but—what is it with you two?'

'Nothing,' she said firmly, because it was nothing, especially after their conversation last night, and Dan was the last person she wanted to talk about. 'Really, he's just a colleague—'

'Don't give me that. I don't believe it for a moment. You were both looking at each other, and the tension between you—well, I don't know, if you're not taking advantage of it you're wasting a golden opportunity, because he is seriously hot!'

She shook her head. 'It's not going to happen.'

'Why on earth not?'

'Because it's more complicated than that.'

She had another bite of the biscuit, but Livvy wasn't going to let it drop.

'How complicated can it be? Crumbs, me and Matt are pretty complicated. It can't be worse than that.'

She wasn't sure, but she wasn't going to discuss it, even with Livvy. She swallowed, brushed the crumbs off her lap and took a drink. She hated lying, but…

'I'm not interested in a relationship, Livvy, and especially not with someone I have to work with. We're barely even friends.' And that was the way it was going to have to stay.

'If you say so.'

'I do. Mind if I have a cuddle with your little bundle of joy?' she said, changing the subject firmly, and Livvy smiled her understanding and handed the baby over. She settled her in the crook of her arm, and Esme immediately stirred and turned her head towards her, rose-bud lips pursed, and she felt the familiar tug of yearning.

'Oh, dear, I think someone's hungry,' she murmured, and handed her back, leaving her arms empty.

Always empty, with an ache that nothing could fill.

She needed to get out of there, so she glanced at her phone. 'Oh, goodness, is that the time?

I need to fly. I've got so much to do.' Which wasn't exactly a lie, more an exaggeration.

Livvy reached out a hand and squeezed her arm. 'Thank you so much, for everything. You were amazing yesterday. You made me feel so safe.'

'That's my job,' she said with a smile, and bent and kissed Livvy's cheek, laid her hand lightly on the baby's soft, downy head and left them to it before she started to cry.

Work seemed odd without Georgie there.

Odd, but no less stressful, because it was a crazy day with one intervention after another requiring his attention, on top of a gynae theatre list that had left him wrung out.

The list kicked off with removal of a cervical cancer in a thirty-two-year-old woman who had been trying to start a family without success. She'd missed the last two smear tests because she'd been on holiday, or too busy, and by the time she'd had one it had gone too far for a cone biopsy. He'd hoped to be able to save at least the top of her uterus in the long and complex operation, but when he opened her up it was worse than the scans had revealed.

Nevertheless, although she lost her uterus and a lot of associated structures and with them any hope of carrying a baby, it hadn't spread to her lymph nodes so at least she now stood a chance of making a full recovery. And he'd managed to salvage her ovaries by doing a transposition, re-siting them high up in her abdomen out of the field of any potential radiotherapy, so at least he'd not plunged her headlong into the menopause.

And there was always surrogacy. Small mercies…

She was followed in Theatre by a few routine ops, but his mind kept going back to her and he felt it acutely, and of course there was no one there to decompress with. Well, no one he knew, at least. Only Jo, his registrar, who'd assisted, and Patrick, who was observing and who'd also found it really hard to deal with, so he ended up counselling him instead.

Then he had to break the news to his cancer patient and her husband that she'd lost her uterus. It hadn't been unexpected, but she closed her eyes and tears slid down her cheeks, and he was gutted for her.

'Looking on the bright side, at least you haven't dumped me into the land of hot flushes, and there's always the possibility of harvesting my eggs, I guess,' she said with a brave attempt at a smile.

'There is,' he said gently. 'But give yourself time. I'll come and see you again tomorrow, and we'll talk about where we go from here, OK?'

She nodded, her smile wobbling, and as he walked away he heard a sob and the sound of her husband's voice trying to soothe her. Was that how Georgie felt? As if everything she'd looked forward to in life had been ripped away?

On the way out he dropped into the antenatal ward to check if he was needed, and was confronted by a frantic midwife who had an exhausted mother, a distressed baby, and Patrick on her hands.

'I was about to call you, Patrick's totally out of his depth and she needs intervention. I've done an episiotomy already, but I think she needs forceps, it's a bit high for the ventouse and he just can't do it and there's nobody else,' she said, and Dan gave an inward sigh.

'Let me have a go,' he said, and introduced himself to the exhausted woman, had a look at what was going on and within five minutes he'd lifted the baby out using forceps, and she had a healthy, squalling baby in her arms.

It was a lovely way to end the day, but by the time he left it was almost eight, and he walked home, opened the door and saw Georgie's jumper, waiting for him to return it.

He stood and stared at it. He could take it

to work tomorrow. Or he could walk round to hers now, and drop it off. It was a beautiful evening, and frankly he needed something to do to chase away the shadows of the challenging day, so he ran upstairs, showered to wash away all traces of the hospital, pulled on jeans and a shirt and headed out, jumper in hand.

She answered the door in bare feet, a loose cotton shirt and cropped trousers with grubby knees. Her fair hair was scooped up in an untidy ponytail, gold tendrils escaping to frame her face, and he felt a rush of warmth, coupled with some good old-fashioned lust.

So much for friendship...

Typical. She was hot and sweaty, her clothes were dirty from gardening and she had no idea what her hair was doing, but Dan was standing there, her jumper in his hands, and he held it out to her with a wry smile.

'You left this behind yesterday,' he said without preamble, and she took it from him.

'I know, I realised this morning. You didn't need to bring it, tomorrow would have done.' She studied him for a moment, saw the shadows in his eyes and forgot about how she looked. 'Tough day?' she murmured.

He gave a short huff of what might possibly have been laughter, and nodded. 'Is it that obvious?'

'Absolutely. You look knackered. Want to come in?'

'No, you don't want me here. I'm not good company tonight.'

She tutted at him and stepped back. 'Don't be silly, I don't need entertaining. Come in and have a drink in the garden.'

He hesitated, then nodded. 'OK—but just one, and no alcohol.'

He stepped inside, shut the door and followed her into the kitchen, and she looked at him again. 'Have you eaten today?'

He laughed again, this time more recognisably, and gave her a wry smile. 'Not so you'd notice. I had a sandwich at some point this afternoon. Not sure when. But you don't need to feed me, a glass of something cold would be lovely. I can cook when I get home, I've got a fridge full of food.'

'Do you really want to be doing that? You're here now and I've got the last of the leftover chilli in the freezer, and some tortilla chips. Will that do?'

He held her eyes for a long moment, then gave a weary chuckle. 'That would be amazing. Thank you.'

She turned her back on him, digging out the

chilli from the freezer, hugely conscious of his presence behind her in the small kitchen.

She could almost feel the warmth of his body drifting in the air, along with the scent of his shampoo or body wash. Subtle, masculine and doing nothing whatsoever for her peace of mind or their decision to be simple friends. Nothing simple about it.

At all. And as for her not wanting him there...

She put the chilli in the microwave, found the tortilla chips and the yogurt, grated some cheese and turned to find him propped against the wall, arms folded and staring into space with a sombre expression on his face.

She handed him a cold alcohol-free beer out of the fridge and met his eyes. 'Come on, let's take this outside,' she said, and piling everything onto a tray she led him through the living room and out into her tiny courtyard garden.

She had a little bistro set out there, and she plonked the tray on it, pushed it towards him and watched him eat mechanically. She waited until he'd finished and put his fork down, then she broke the silence.

'Want to talk about it?'

He met her eyes, smiled wearily and shook his head.

'Not really. I'm not sure I've got the energy.'

'Did you lose a patient?'

He shook his head again. 'No, and actually in some ways it was a good day. Bit of a curate's egg, really, but my gynae list kicked off with a young woman with cervical cancer that was diagnosed late. She's lost her uterus, but I did a transposition so I've managed to save her ovaries and there's a good chance she'll live, but it wasn't nice having to tell her that she'll never be able to carry a child. I think she pretty much knew it would happen, but there was a tiny shred of hope and I had to trash it. That was tough—but I don't have to tell you that.'

She felt her eyes prickle, and blinked. 'No. It's not something anybody wants to know, but I'm glad you've given her a chance of survival, and maybe a chance of a baby with a surrogate.'

'Yeah. Me, too. It was pretty major surgery and the prognosis is still guarded, but I've referred her to Oncology so it's all down to them now. She's only thirty-two, two years younger than me.'

And a year older than her. What a tragedy. 'You needed to talk to someone,' she said, and he laughed.

'I did. I ended up counselling Patrick after

we finished in Theatre. He was observing the gynae ops, and it was a tough list with that young woman and it got to him a bit, but that's to be expected; he's only just started his obs and gynae rotation a week and a bit ago, and it's a steep learning curve. We've all been there. He just needs some experience under his belt. He'll be a good GP, I'm sure, and he's a great listener, but he's not a surgeon by any stretch of the imagination. And then when I was leaving I had to rescue him again.'

'Now what?'

He laughed, but it sounded weary and a bit jaded. 'A poor exhausted woman who just didn't have the reserves left to push the baby out. It was virtually there, Kat had done an episiotomy, but she still couldn't find the strength and she needed help, and Patrick was right out of his depth.'

'Oh, poor Kat. So what did you do? Use the ventouse?'

'No, it was too high, so I used forceps and it was all done and dusted in five minutes, but I could have done without it. Still, it was a training opportunity and it ended on a high, but it was a long day, one of those days that we all get from time to time.'

They did, and everyone felt the way he was obviously feeling. One of the drawbacks of being in a caring profession, and as for not getting involved, tell it to the fairies. They all did. Some just dealt with it better than others.

'I'm sorry I wasn't there for you.'

His eyes flicked back to hers and he gave a wry smile.

'Don't be. I'm a big boy now, I can cope. Anyway, enough of me. How was your day? Done anything interesting?'

She laughed at that. 'Oh, riveting. I stripped the bed, put the sheets in the washing machine, watered the plants, went and saw Livvy and took her some presents, came back via the shops to pick up some food and I've been out here mostly. I hung out the washing, did a bit of pot tweaking, deadheaded the rose, such as it is, and then I read a book.'

'That sounds lovely,' he said with a touch of envy in his voice. 'How's Livvy?'

'Doing well. Baby's gorgeous, breastfeeding's going well, so all good.'

'And you?'

She laughed again, a tiny huff, and gave him what had to be a twisted little smile. 'Dan, really, I'm fine. I deal with it every single day. It's what I do. I can handle it.'

His mouth was wry. 'Yeah, and I know how that goes.'

He looked away, glancing at her garden. 'It's

lovely out here. I don't know what's in your pots, but they smell heavenly and they look gorgeous. It works really well.'

'Thank you. It does, but it gets really hot out here by the end of the day and I spend my life watering, so it's a lot of work. Your garden's so full and lush and pretty, and I'm really envious of your lawn and the bench in the shade under that tree, but this is fine for me, I'm happy with it. I couldn't cope with yours.'

He chuckled at that. 'It remains to be seen whether I can. I've only been there a week and Tom left it immaculate, but it's rapidly becoming my favourite room in the house—if you can call it a room.'

She could imagine that. Not that there was anything wrong with the house itself, from what little she'd seen of it, but it was simply furnished, white from end to end, and unlike the garden it was very much a blank canvas waiting for him to put his stamp on it.

If he did. She had the feeling he might not bother, not if he was planning on moving.

'So what kind of house do you want to buy when you sell your other one?' she asked, and he shrugged.

'I don't know. It depends. I haven't really looked, so I've got no idea what the local housing stock is like.'

'Pricey, mostly,' she said with a smile. 'This is very modest but it stretched me to the limit.'

'There's nothing wrong with it. It's a nice house.'

'I think so, and it suits me, but I don't think it would suit you, not with this tiny scrap of garden. Men always seem to want to cut grass.'

He laughed for the first time that day with a bit of genuine amusement. 'Bit of a sweeping generalisation,' he said, but he didn't argue, so she carried on.

'So where would you want to be? In town? In a village just outside, buried in the countryside up to your neck in nettles?'

'Probably not the nettles,' he said with a wry grin.

'OK, no nettles. How about overlooking the sea on the clifftop, or down by the yacht harbour near the river mouth? That's nice, and one of the ED consultants lives there. Livvy and Matt are on the clifftop in a gorgeous modernist house near Ed and Annie. You met Ed on your first day, he was looking after Susie's baby. That's the prime spot if you want a stunning sea view, but they're eye-wateringly expensive. If you like Victorian grandeur there's the old part of town. Ben and Daisy Walker have a massive house there stuffed with original features, so do Jake and Emily Stratton.

You know them, they job-share in our department. And Nick and Liv Jarvis live not far from here but in a much more sensible house. You must have met them, too. He's an obstetrician and Liv's a midwife.'

'Yes, I've met most of them. So they're all pretty local, then?'

'They are. It makes being on call easier, and it's also a great community. Lots of social stuff. It's like one big family.'

He nodded slowly. 'I'm sure. It sounds like there's lots of variety to choose from when I get round to it, but I'm quite happy in the cottage for now. There's no hurry and it's not like I'm short of space.'

He glanced at his phone, drained the last dreg of his beer and put the can down. 'I need to go. It's getting late, and I've no doubt got another killer day tomorrow. I'm on take.'

'Oh, joy. I'm doing a double shift tomorrow. Seven till nine. I can hardly wait.'

He chuckled and tipped his head on one side. 'I'll be there if you need anything.'

Her heart gave a sudden thud and she ignored it. 'What, like my peanut butter opened?' she said lightly, and his mouth twitched.

'Something like that.'

He unravelled his legs and stood up, and

she got to her feet and followed him to the front door.

And then they stalled, tension hanging in the air.

'I'm glad you came round,' she said, breaking the suddenly loaded silence.

'So am I. I'll try not to make it a habit.'

She laughed. 'Feel free. I'm never doing anything else.'

He hesitated a moment, then reeled her in against his chest for a gentle hug. 'Thank you,' he murmured into her hair. 'For feeding me again, giving me a shoulder to cry on—or whinge on, at least—you're a star.'

She wrapped her arms around him and hugged him back, her head resting briefly on his shoulder as she breathed in the scent of him, warm and clean and enticing. Too enticing. She let go and stepped away out of reach.

'You're welcome. You can return the favour when I need it.'

'It'll be my pleasure.' He smiled and opened the door. 'I'll see you in the morning. Sleep well.'

'And you.'

She closed the door behind him, rested against it for a moment and then shrugged herself away, gathered up all the things in the garden, loaded the dishwasher and went to bed.

It wasn't made, of course, because she'd washed the sheets that morning to get rid of the scent of his skin so she could stop fantasising about him all night…

She pulled fresh linen out of the airing cupboard, made the bed and crawled into it. Much better. Well, not better, but better for her peace of mind.

Except she went to sleep and dreamed about him anyway, which did nothing for her peace of mind at all.

He shouldn't have hugged her.

Stupid, stupid thing to do—but she'd been just there, right under his nose, with her messy hair and her gentle smile, and he hadn't been able to resist the urge.

He was glad he hadn't. It had been good to hold her. So good. And to talk to her. She was right, he'd needed to decompress, and she understood, knew what he was talking about, felt the same pressures and responsibilities. And one day no doubt he'd be able to return the favour.

He let himself into his cottage, walked straight through it and out into the garden, kicking off his shoes and grabbing a cold drink on the way. There was a white rose trained against the fence, the blooms almost luminous in the dark, and he headed past it to the bench under the tree, the grass cool and damp under his feet, and thought of her little paved courtyard garden filled with pots, and how she'd said she loved this garden. He loved it, too. It was a refuge from reality, a kind of sanctuary, and he'd be sorry to leave it when the time came.

It was dark now, with just the light of the moon to guide him, and the air was heavy with scent from the plants beside the bench. He didn't know what they were, but Georgie might know. He thought he recognised the scent from her garden. He'd have to ask her next time she was here.

He closed his eyes, letting the day fall away from him and the peace steal in to take its place, and all around him he could hear the rustling of tiny creatures. There was even an owl in the distance.

Bliss.

Maybe he needed to buy a hammock and sling it between the tree and the fence— except it might pull the fence over, but he could get one in a frame.

Or just go to bed.

He hoisted himself off the bench and headed inside.

* * *

She hardly saw him the next day.

He was rushed off his feet, she had two women in established labour that she was moving between and another being induced that she was monitoring for progress, and the day flew by.

Before she knew it her shift was over, and she walked home, let herself in, made some beans on toast and went out to the garden. It seemed empty without him, and it was oddly lonely.

That annoyed her. She'd never been lonely before, so why should she be lonely now? Ridiculous.

She ate her meal, watered the pots and went to bed, and again she could feel his presence. Or absence, more accurately.

She really needed to get a grip.

For the next two weeks they were like ships in the night.

He helped her with an awkward breech delivery, but apart from that she scarcely saw him because she had a week of nights in the middle of it, which was a killer. She even had to get Patrick to wrestle the top off her peanut butter jar, but at least he was capable of that. He told her that Dan had taken him under his wing and was mentoring him, so she had hopes for his progress. There was plenty of room for it.

But as for her and Dan—well, at least she was getting used to seeing him around, and with enough practice maybe her heart would stop doing stupid things every time she heard his voice. Not that he was unfriendly, far from it, he was just as busy as she was.

Then after her run of nights and her days off, she got sent down to his antenatal clinic because they were short of midwives and it was miraculously quiet on the labour ward, so she ended up working with him.

A new patient who was there for her twelve-week scan was worried sick because she'd had a little bleeding, so the first thing Georgie did was try and listen for the baby's heartbeat, but she couldn't find it.

'OK, I can't seem to locate it but that could just be the position it's in, so let's do a pregnancy test.'

She took a test strip out of her pocket where she'd put a few in case she needed them, stripped the wrapper off and dipped the strip into the urine sample the woman had brought with her, then waited until the first and then the second line appeared.

They didn't have to wait many seconds, and she smiled at her relieved patient.

'Well, it still says you're pregnant, so that's good news. I think our next move needs to be the scan. You're here for one anyway, so let me go and bump you up the queue and I'll come back to you in a moment. The consultant might want to have a look at you as well.'

She went out and tapped on Dan's door, and he opened it instantly, as if he'd been on the way out.

'Hello, stranger,' he said with a smile. 'Do you need me?'

That again…

'If you're not busy. I've got a worried first-time mum. She's twelve weeks, had a bit of bleeding, I can't hear a heartbeat but the pregnancy test says she's pregnant and I think her placenta is probably in the way. She's in for a scan. Do you want me to get that done first, or do you want to have a listen? There's a queue for the scan.'

'Let's do both,' he said, and followed her back in.

'Hi, my name's Daniel Blake, I'm the consultant in charge of your care. Do you mind if I have a listen to your baby?'

She shook her head, still looking worried, and he pulled his Doppler out of his pocket, wiggled it around for a minute, tried again in a different position and just when Georgie was giving up hope the room was filled with the wonderful whooshing sound of the baby's heart.

'There we go,' he said with a smile, and the woman burst into tears of relief. Dan slid the Doppler back into his pocket, handed her a tissue and winked at Georgie.

He opened his mouth to say something, and she gave him a look and he just grinned and walked out without a word, but she was too relieved to be cross that he'd found it and she hadn't.

That wasn't what mattered, and in the end the scan was fine, so the woman was sent off with her next appointment booked and a photo of her perfectly healthy baby. The rest of the clinic was busy but routine, with no dramas or crises, and she ended her shift only an hour late.

She went into the locker room to change, found the pregnancy tests strips still in her pocket and put them in her locker, then changed her clothes, dropping the scrubs into the laundry bin. Then she pulled out her bag and a tampon fell out. She bent down and picked it up, then stared at it thoughtfully.

Was her period overdue?

She wasn't sure. Her cycle wasn't an issue, so she never really bothered to make a note, but her periods usually started on a Tuesday, and it was Thursday.

Her heart gave a dull thud and she stared at it for another moment, then put it and the test strips in her bag and shut her locker.

There was no way she could be pregnant— was there? Surely not.

But all the way home her heart was racing, and the first thing she did once she'd closed the front door was run upstairs to the bathroom to do the test.

How could a minute be so long?

She perched on the edge of the bath, staring at the little strip and not quite sure what she wanted to see, one line or two.

One appeared instantly, to show the test was working. Not that anything else was going to happen—

Another line? Really? And a strong, dark line, too, not some vague little shadow.

She got up, her legs like jelly, and walked slowly out of the bathroom, sank down onto the bed and stared blankly at the test strip.

How could she possibly be pregnant? Dan had said it was a tiny tear, and she and Mark had tried for *years*. How could she be? Unless they'd just been incompatible, but even so…

She slid a hand down over her board-flat tummy. Was there really a baby in there? Dan's baby?

Please, no.

Please, yes!

But...

She'd have to tell him. Not yet, though. It might have been a fluke. She'd do another test in a while.

And then another one, until all the tests were used up.

Four of them *couldn't* be wrong.

She started to cry, great tearing sobs welling up from deep inside her where the pain she'd hidden for so long had festered like poison, and then the tears died away, leaving only joy.

She was having a baby, the thing she'd always dreamed of and had given up hoping for.

And Dan was going to be a father.

How on earth was she going to tell him?

CHAPTER FIVE

HE HADN'T SEEN her for ages.

Not really, not to speak to, apart from over that antenatal patient yesterday, because she'd been on nights. He told himself it was a good thing, they needed a little distance, but actually it didn't feel good, and in a strange way he missed her.

And he still owed her dinner, even if that had started as a joke. A real dinner, in a proper restaurant like Zacharelli's on the seafront, not whatever either of them could pull together.

No. Not Zacharelli's. It would feel altogether too much like a date, and that was dangerous.

A picnic, then, or supper in a pub. Nick Jarvis had talked about the pub on the other side of the river, overlooking the harbour and with great river views. Was that still too dateish? Because he didn't want it to be. No matter how much he wanted her, and he absolutely did, he didn't want a relationship.

Well, not that sort. Too messy, too much potential for hurt and disappointment, and altogether too complicated with them working together.

How would they both feel if it all went wrong?

Awkward. Hideously awkward. It just couldn't be allowed to happen. But they could be friends, couldn't they? If they could make it work–

His phone pinged in his pocket, and he pulled it out and glanced at the screen. Georgia.

Can we grab a coffee?

He laughed. Coffee. That was it, perfect for a quick catchup. If there was ever a time when they were both free...

You read my mind. How about now? I'm miraculously free

It was a slight exaggeration, but her reply was instant.

Can you give me five minutes?

He checked the time. Just about, although it'd be a squeeze.

Sure. Park Café in ten?

Perfect!

He slid his phone back into his pocket, finished off what he was doing and sprinted through the park, catching up with her at the door.

'Well, hello, stranger,' he said, following her in, and she turned and smiled.

Or sort of smiled. There was something different about her that he couldn't quite work out. Something—guarded? He cocked his head on one side and studied her.

'Are you all right?'

She smiled again, but it didn't quite reach her eyes. 'Yes, I'm fine. Why?'

'I don't know. I haven't seen you to speak to for ages. Are we OK?'

'Of course. Why wouldn't we be?'

'I don't know.' But he had a gut feeling something was wrong. 'Have I done something to upset you?'

'No, of course you haven't, but as you say it's been ages, so I thought you were avoiding *me* for some reason.'

So that was it. Relieved, he shook his head. 'No, of course I'm not. I'm just stupidly busy.' He hesitated, then confessed, 'I almost dropped in last night on my way home to say hi, but I didn't know what you were doing and I didn't want to presume.'

'Ah, no. I was busy last night,' she said, and turned to the person behind the counter. Skinny decaf cappuccino, please. Dan?'

'I'll have a double espresso, please. Since when did you drink decaf?' he added to her.

'I often have decaf,' she said, and turned and picked up a gooey pastry. 'Just in case I don't get a lunch break,' she said.

'Good plan,' he said, and reached past her into the grab-and-go chiller and picked up a coronation chicken wrap.

By the time he turned back she was at the till, card at the ready.

'My turn,' she said firmly, and paid, picked up the tray and headed out into the sunshine.

It was a glorious day again, and she went to the same bench that they'd sat on before, set the tray down in the middle and picked up her coffee, wondering where to start.

'So, how's it going? Settling in?' she asked, her voice sounding a tiny bit forced to her ears, and he nodded slowly.

'Yes, I think so. It's all good—well, so far. How are things with you?'

How could she answer that? *My world's*

just turned upside down, but apart from that it's fine?

'OK. Stupidly busy, like you. How's the lawn mowing going?'

Oh, that's so inane...

'Good. Well, so far, but it hasn't rained a lot so it's not really growing. It'll be more of a challenge when it does.'

They fell silent, then—

'Dan, I—'

'How do you—'

They'd spoken together, and she laughed and waved for him to go ahead, glad of the reprieve.

'I was going to say, how do you fancy supper at mine one night? It's my turn and I was thinking—oh, now what?' he asked, pulling out his pager. He swore, got to his feet and shrugged helplessly. 'Sorry, I've got to go, I'm needed in the ED. I'll pop in tonight on my way home and we can sort something out. OK?'

'Sure.' She smiled, but it faded as she watched him go, heading towards the ED entrance, his coffee and wrap untouched. She'd take them up with her and put them in the ward kitchen, but for now she was going to drink her decaf coffee, eat her sticky, sugar-loaded pastry and regroup.

Just as well his pager had gone off when it had, because she'd been all ready to blurt it out, and if she'd just dumped that on him in a public place, it would have been really unfair.

Not as tricky as if he'd dropped in last night when she'd just found out, though. That was a narrow escape, because she'd needed time to come to terms with it herself before she dealt with his emotions. And goodness knows what they were going to be.

Better tonight.

And that would give her a little more time to work out what to say.

In the end it was easy.

He turned up at almost eight, apologised for the time, thanked her for putting his lunch in the fridge, and then he looked at her closely and asked if she was all right.

'You looked a bit strained this morning, and you weren't yourself. Is everything OK?'

She felt her shoulders slump, and gave up trying to word it any other way than the obvious.

'That depends what you call OK.' She took a deep breath, closed the front door and turned to face him. 'I'm pregnant,' she said quietly, and she watched the blood drain from his face.

He said nothing for an age, but his face said

it all. Shock, disbelief, anger—with her, or himself, she wasn't sure—and then he shook his head.

'No. No, I can't do this again,' he said rawly, and turned without another word, yanked open the front door and walked out.

What? She'd spent the whole day trying to work out how to tell him, running through potential conversations in her head, dreading his reaction, but this was the last thing she'd expected, the absolute last thing.

She stood motionless, staring open-mouthed through the open door as he strode away out of sight, and then the dam burst.

She sank down onto the bottom step, great wrenching sobs tearing themselves out of her chest, and she clung to the banisters and sobbed her heart out. How could he do that to her? Walk away without even talking about it? It was his baby, too, his condom that had torn—and her denial that she needed emergency contraception. She'd been so adamant that it was unnecessary, and now...

'Oh, what have I done?' she whispered, and another wave of guilt and sorrow swept over her. She buried her face in her hands and wept again, the endless tears dribbling through her fingers and running down her wrists, and then she heard a car door slam and the front door close, felt gentle hands wrap around her shoulders and the nudge of a hip against hers, his arms easing her up against his chest.

'Georgia, don't cry,' he said, his voice rough and raw with emotion. 'I can't bear that I made you cry.'

'Why did you go like that? Why did you leave me?'

She felt the shaky breath of his sigh against her skin. 'I just needed some air, but I shouldn't have gone, I know that, and I'm sorry.'

'No, I'm sorry. This is all my fault,' she wept, but he hushed her and rocked her against his warm, solid body.

'No, it's not all your fault. If it's anyone's fault, it's mine. If I hadn't stayed...'

But he had, and that was her fault, and it set her off again.

She felt a gentle hand stroke her hair. 'Come on, Georgie, stop crying and let's talk about this calmly and rationally.'

She sniffed and scrubbed her face with her hands, easing away from him. 'What is there to talk about? I'm pregnant, it's your baby— what else is there to say? You said it all. You can't do it again. What more is there?'

'There's a lot more. Well, a lot I have to say, anyway, starting with a proper apology for running away just now. And I could make all sorts of excuses, but that wouldn't be fair. I still shouldn't have left you.'

'I thought you were angry with me.'

'I am a bit. I'm more angry with myself, but above all I'm worried about you, and about the baby. It's too late for recriminations. What's happened has happened, for whatever reason, and we need to move forward.'

'I didn't lie to you,' she said, finally lifting her head and meeting his eyes. 'I honestly believed this could never happen. We'd tried for years and nothing had happened and I knew it wasn't him, but maybe it was just incompatibility. If I'd had even the slightest doubt that I could get pregnant I would have done something about it immediately.'

'Would you? Even though you've always wanted a baby?'

She nodded.

'Yes, I would, because I knew you didn't. It was a one-off, we weren't in a relationship, and you told me the next day that you had issues, so I knew you wouldn't want a baby...'

'No. I didn't want to get you pregnant. I never said I didn't want a baby.'

Hadn't he? Probably not, in so many words, but you couldn't have one without the other...

'Maybe not, but you certainly wouldn't want one with a random stranger, not after what you'd gone through—although I suppose that might be easier. If you didn't love someone it wouldn't hurt as much if it all went wrong.'

'That's not true. Being responsible for anyone's death or suffering is always going to hurt.'

He smiled, but it was a sad effort and it made her want to cry again.

He must have seen, because he gave her shoulder a little squeeze. 'Don't worry about me, I'm fine. You need to go and wash your face and dry your eyes, and we'll go to mine and have something to eat and talk about this, OK?'

She nodded, and he got to his feet, pulled her up and hugged her, and it felt so good she just wanted to stay there, but he dropped his arms and stepped back, and she went into the cloakroom, splashed her face, looked at herself in the mirror and could have cried again.

So many tears…

She patted her face dry, went out and found him standing in the living room, hands rammed in his pockets, staring out into the garden.

He'd said he was fine, but he didn't look it. He looked as if he was staring into the abyss, and she felt another wash of guilt.

I can't do this again…

'I could feed us,' she suggested, but he shook his head.

'I've got stuff in the fridge that needs eating. If we go back to mine I can cook for you and we can eat it in the garden while we talk. It's more private than yours, and it's cooler.'

She couldn't argue with that, and she realised she didn't want to, so she nodded, picked up her bag and her keys, set the alarm and followed him out.

She looked awful.

Utterly gutted, and he had no idea what she'd want to do.

Would she keep it? He had no idea, but it was her decision to make, even though it'd kill him to stand back and let it happen. Her right, her choice. Her baby.

He'd brought the car back with him almost the minute he'd got home, and it was hitched up on the kerb outside. He drove them back to his, ushered her in and walked through to the kitchen, crunching over the broken china.

She stopped at the threshold and stared at it. 'What happened?' she asked, her voice shocked, and he gave a short huff of laughter.

If you could remotely call it that.

'I lost it a bit, but I'm OK now.'

'Are you?' she asked, and searched his eyes,

her own worried. 'Are you really? Or are you still angry?'

He smiled at her, but it was a sad effort and he could see she wasn't convinced.

'Only with myself,' he said honestly, surprised to realise it was true. 'I just want to talk to you, Georgia, work out where we go from here, how we deal with this. But let's get supper under way because I'm starving. What do you fancy?'

'I don't know. What have you got?'

'All sorts. Why don't you look in the fridge and I'll sweep this up?'

He left her examining the food, cleared up the mess he'd made when he'd hurled the mug across the room, and then stood beside her at the open fridge door.

'Thoughts?'

'Something healthy. The sea bream fillets, maybe, with new potatoes and a salad?'

'Sounds good. Why don't I get you a drink and then I'll start cooking?'

It only took him a few minutes, and while he cooked she sat on the bench under the tree and sipped her sparkling water and breathed in the scent of the nicotiana and night-scented stocks, with the grass cool under her bare feet and her mind in turmoil.

What did he mean by 'deal with this'? It seemed to imply that there were choices, but to her there were no choices, and only one possible option.

Yes, it might not have been planned, and he might not want to have anything at all to do with it, but for her this unexpected pregnancy was nothing short of a miracle.

But it was his baby, too. Would he reject his own child?

No. He'd said he only wanted her not to be pregnant, not that he didn't want a baby. So what did he want, and what did he really feel?

I can't do this again...

Her hands slid down, curling over her baby as if to shield it from harm, and she closed her eyes and told herself to breathe.

He dished up, carried the plates to the door and stopped.

She was sitting on the bench, eyes closed, hands held against her abdomen in a protective gesture that wrenched at his gut, and his heart went out to her.

That was his fault. All of this was his fault, and there was nothing he could do to turn back the clock and take it away.

It was up to him to make it right, in whatever way he could, no matter what the cost to him personally or financially.

He put the plates down on the table and walked over to her. 'Hey. It's ready,' he said gently, and she looked up and smiled.

'Thank you.'

She got to her feet and walked back with him, and they sat and ate in silence, and then finally she pushed back her plate, met his eyes and said, 'What do you want me to do?'

He didn't pretend not to understand.

'It's not my decision,' he said.

'That doesn't stop you having an opinion.'

'My opinion is irrelevant. As long as you're carrying it, this is your baby. Whatever happens, it has to be your decision, and whatever you decide, I'll stand by you.'

Even if it broke his heart.

She stared at him for the longest time. 'Do you really mean that, or are you just saying it because you feel you should?'

'No, I really mean it.'

'What about your "I can't do this again" comment? What was that about? Because you weren't standing by me then, by any stretch of the imagination.'

He shook his head. 'I was in shock. I didn't mean it, Georgia, and I'm really sorry I said it. I was just poleaxed, but of course I can do it. I'm here for you, whatever you want, I promise.'

'Honestly?'

'Honestly.'

'OK.' She held his eyes. 'I want to keep it,' she said, watching him carefully, and he felt the air go out of him like a punctured balloon.

'Are you sure? You're not just saying that for me?'

She shook her head. 'No. I've wanted a baby for ever, and I never thought it would happen. I'm still not sure I believe it, but I'm more than ready for it. And I can do it. I've got a good support network, so I won't be alone—'

'You won't be alone,' he assured her. 'I'll be there for you, Georgia. Always. And for the baby. We can do this together, somehow.'

Somehow? What did that mean, exactly?

And—together. What did *that* mean? Together as in together, or just shared decision-making? And as for parenting...

She had no idea. 'So how are we going to do this?' she asked, and he shrugged.

'Honestly? I don't know. I suggest we play it by ear, take it a day at a time.'

'OK. That sounds good.'

What does together mean?

'So are we going to tell everyone?' she asked him.

'Everyone?'

'Our colleagues, friends.'

'No. No, not yet. Nobody needs to know.'

'And how does that work? Because it's going to become obvious pretty soon and they're all going to want to know whose it is.'

'Do you have to tell them?'

'Dan, they're my *friends*! Be realistic.'

'OK. You need to tell your friends.'

'And how about colleagues? How about Ben Walker? Because he's your clinical lead, and his wife is a friend of mine. And he will ask, I know he will, and I'll either have to tell him or lie, which I don't want to do.'

He frowned. 'No. I realise that.'

'So—what do I say to people? Do I tell them you're the father, or are we going to pretend we've had nothing to do with each other? Because that simply won't work. I'm not that good a liar, and I don't want to have to lie about this.'

He sighed and scrubbed a hand through his hair, and she could understand his dilemma. 'OK, you have to tell Ben, and your friends, but not everyone. At least not yet. Not till your scan.'

'No, I agree. And this—together thing you

talked about. What did you mean by that? What kind of together?'

He held her eyes for a long moment, then looked away.

'I don't know. I just know this baby is my responsibility, and so are you now, and I don't shirk my responsibilities.'

'I'm not your responsibility!'

'Yes, you are. Your health and welfare, at least, until the end of your pregnancy and probably longer, so—whatever you want from me, whatever you want for us, I'll consider it. Money, marriage—whatever.'

Marriage? She considered that for a second, but no more, because the last thing she needed after a man who'd left her because she couldn't give him a child was a man who would only be with her *because* she was having a child.

She could understand where he was coming from, but that didn't mean she had to hand over her own responsibility, and she wouldn't. It wasn't necessary.

'I don't want anything from you, Dan, and certainly not marriage,' she said truthfully. 'This is my fault, not yours. I knew the condom had torn, I hadn't had any fertility tests, and common sense would have dictated that I take emergency contraception just to be on the safe side, but I didn't because I genuinely didn't believe I needed to, and that was a mistake. So you're off the hook.'

'I don't want to be off the hook,' he said, to her surprise. 'This is my baby too, and I really want to be involved, from now onwards, for ever.' She felt a wave of relief, and then he added, 'I'd like to supervise your care, too, but obviously I can't.'

She felt her eyes widen, her relief gone.

'No, you can't. It's totally unethical, and for good reasons.'

'I get that, but I would like to be involved where possible, scans and that sort of thing, so I suppose when it comes to that point people will need to know I'm the father.'

He didn't sound thrilled by that. 'Is that a problem for you?' she asked bluntly. 'That people will know you slept with me?'

'No, of course it isn't. In fact it might be good if people already thought we were together by then.'

'What, so it doesn't look as if I'm such a slut?'

He gave a sharp sigh. 'You're not a slut, not by any stretch of the imagination, Georgia, and it takes two, so what does that make me?' He shrugged. 'I'm not ashamed of what we did, and if it makes it easier for you with your friends that we're in a relationship, then tell them that. I'm fine with it.'

'It would be a lie, though,' she said, after a long pause, and then met his eyes. 'Unless we were.'

He looked away, gave another shrug, maybe slightly bewildered as he groped his way through it. Just like her, then. 'We are, in a way. And maybe we should be. It's a long road. Maybe we should travel it together.'

She shook her head. 'No. It's not a good enough reason,' she said, quoting his own words back at him, and something odd happened in his eyes before he looked away.

'No, probably not,' he said, but he sounded almost sorry about that and she wondered what he really did think, what he really did want. Apart from fulfilling his responsibilities, which was something Mark had never understood.

'I don't think we need to lie,' she said eventually. 'Discretion would be good, and I'd be grateful if you didn't talk about us to anyone, and of course I'll share my handheld notes with you, they're about your child, but I don't want you hovering over me like a cross between a helicopter and a guardian angel, watching my every move for the next eight months, because it isn't necessary and it'll do my head in. I'm quite capable of looking after myself and lots of women do this perfectly well on their own.'

He frowned at that, but he nodded, and she realised she'd hit a nerve.

'Oh, Dan, I'm sorry. That was tactless, but I'm fine. I'm fit and well, I know what I'm doing, I know what to look out for, and I know you don't want a relationship really. Nor do I. Certainly not one based on duty and guilt and a misplaced sense of valour.'

'That's not what this is about.'

'Yes, it is. Of course it is. What else could it be about?' She gave a weary shrug. 'Look, I'm sorry, but I'm tired, and I think we've both got enough to think about for now. There's no rush, we don't have to do anything at all for a few more weeks, and if the situation changes, we'll look at it again. But for now let's just do what we said and take it one day at a time, please?'

He nodded slowly, his face more sombre than she'd ever seen it, and then he met her eyes.

'OK. I'll run you home.'

'There's no need.'

'Yes, there is. You're tired, so am I, and I'm not letting you walk home alone, so do me a favour and don't argue about it, please. I haven't got the energy for it.'

She gave a soft laugh. 'Well, since you put it so nicely...'

He rolled his eyes. 'Sorry. I'm just a bit...'

'I know. I am too. Come on, then, drive me home, if you insist.'

One day at a time.

That was harder than he'd expected because now, after a fortnight of hardly seeing her, he was falling over her all the time. Ever since she'd dropped the bombshell their shifts seemed to coincide again, and he had no idea what to say, how to talk to her in such a public place.

'How are you?' seemed too loaded. How about, 'You OK?' Better, maybe.

And then a few days into their 'one day at a time' regime, they had a day when they were both on duty and it was quiet. Not that anyone dared to say so, but he picked up on it and suggested a coffee, and his phone pinged instantly.

Ugh. No. Maybe fizzy water.

Oh, dear. See you in the Park Café in five?

He got a thumbs-up in reply, and headed for the café. It was the first time he'd seen her that day, and she looked a little pale. She was sitting on their bench—funny, how they'd claimed it—and she smiled ruefully.

'Can you go in for me? I can't face it. The coffee smells horrendous. Oh, and can I have an apple Danish please? I'm starving.'

'Sure.'

He got to the front of the queue, opened his mouth to ask for his usual double espresso, and switched to tea.

'Here you go. Chilled fizzy water, apple Danish and no, I didn't get myself a coffee.'

'You're a star,' she said, taking a huge bite of the pastry and sighing with what sounded like bliss. Or relief.

'So when did this start?' he asked, and she shrugged.

'I'm not sure. I've been getting pickier, but I'm only just over five weeks. It's very early.'

'Probably twins,' he said with a grin, and her eyes widened.

'Don't even joke about it,' she said, and his heart gave a sudden thud. Early nausea could be an indicator of twin pregnancy, which was why he'd said it, but he'd always thought it was a bit of an old wives' tale. Of course it was.

'It's highly unlikely,' he said, trying to convince himself, and took a bite of his chicken wrap. 'So how are you otherwise?'

She shrugged. 'Fine. Sleepy, hungry but I

can't stand the sight of food—I don't know. How are you? Have you had any more thoughts?'

'About us?' Us… Even the word seemed odd, never mind the concept. 'I'm not sure I have. You?'

'Not really,' she said. 'I still don't really know what you had in mind.'

That dragged a chuckle out of him. 'That makes two of us. The only thing I had in my mind last week was damage limitation. How could I take care of you, make sure you were OK, make sure the baby was OK. I didn't really get beyond that, and I still haven't.'

She tutted softly. 'You don't need to take care of me, Dan. I can take care of myself.'

He nodded slowly. 'Yes. Yes, I know you can—but even so…'

'Look, as soon as I get to twelve weeks I'll have a scan. We can go from there.'

'You need to see a midwife before then, or your GP.'

She rolled her eyes. 'Dan, I AM a midwife! I don't need to see one. I'm taking folic acid, my diet is healthy—don't look at my Danish like that!—and my blood pressure is fine.'

'What about anaemia? You need an FBC.'

'I'm taking an iron supplement, and I'm eating red meat when I can bring myself to cook it, and dark leafy veg and pulses—really, I'm fine. I know you mean well, but please stop fussing. I told you about that helicopter thing.'

He threw up his hands and smiled. 'Sorry, sorry. It's just the doctor in me coming out.'

'No. It's the man who's been racked with guilt for the past ten years,' she said gently, and he swallowed. 'It's OK, I do understand where you're coming from, Dan, and I'm not going to shut you out, but really, you don't need to worry about the baby. I'm doing that for you.'

He nodded, suddenly swamped with all sorts of emotions, but oddly one of them was joy. And so he smiled, and reached out a hand and took hers, giving it a quick squeeze.

'Thank you. I'm sorry if you feel I'm crowding you, and I'll keep out of your way, but ask, please, if there's anything you need. You know where I am.'

Her eyes suddenly seemed to sparkle in the sunlight, and she blinked and turned away, but not before he saw a tear bead on her lashes.

'Thank you,' she murmured. 'And—you don't have to keep out of my way. Feel free to drop in any time you're passing.'

'I might well do that.'

He did, just a few hours later, and she was watering the plants. He only found out because she was en route from the kitchen sink with the watering can when he rang the bell.

'What are you doing? That's heavy.'

'It's not that heavy,' she protested, but he tutted and carried it out and watered the pots for her while she made them both a drink.

'Here. Peppermint tea.'

He took it without comment, sat down and looked at her. 'I've been thinking.'

'Oh, dear,' she teased, and his lips twitched.

'Seriously. You talked this morning about eating if you could bring yourself to cook, so how about if I cook for you and deliver it? Anything you fancy, but so you don't have to handle it. Just hold your nose and eat it.'

She opened her mouth to protest, then shut it, because today she'd been going to cook herself a casserole and she'd ended up with an egg sandwich, and even that had been a struggle once she'd peeled and mashed the egg.

'I can't ask you to do that,' she began, but he cut her off with a raised eyebrow.

'You didn't. I offered. And I'm not helicoptering, before you say it, I'm just being a friend.'

She swallowed. Why did he have to be so nice? Because it would be all too easy to give in and let him look after her.

'It's not really practical,' she said. 'You can't

be expected to ferry it here every night. And anyway, our hours are not always compatible.'

'No, they're not,' he agreed. 'So I thought I could do some batch cooking and you could freeze it. Simple stuff. How does that sound?'

Lonely...

She swallowed again, touched by his thoughtfulness. 'That would be really helpful.'

'OK. Give me some ideas of what you think you might like, and leave it with me. Have you already eaten tonight?'

She laughed. 'If you can call it that. I had an egg sandwich and gagged at the smell.'

He sighed and rolled his eyes. 'Write me a list of things you think you could eat, and I'll go shopping now.'

'But it's late.'

'It's fine. Just do it.'

She sent him off a few minutes later with his list, and he hugged her and dropped a gentle kiss on her cheek on the way out.

'Sleep well. I'll see you tomorrow,' he said, and she nodded, locked the door behind him and headed into the kitchen.

She was suddenly starving, so she had a piece of toast because he was right, an egg sandwich really wasn't adequate, and then went to bed, wrapped in a curious warmth.

Maybe being looked after wouldn't be so bad after all.

Her hand slid up to her cheek and rested there, against his kiss, and she drifted off to sleep with a smile on her face.

CHAPTER SIX

HE GOT TO work early the next morning.

He had a tricky case on his theatre list and he wanted time to check on his patient and reassure her, but it wasn't to be. Sally was on the phone as he arrived, and he was about to walk past the desk when she mouthed 'Hang on,' then finished the call.

'Do you need me?' he asked, and she shook her head.

'I don't but someone does,' she told him, and added quietly, 'Patrick's walked out.'

His heart sank. 'Walked out?'

'Yes. Said it was all too much, he was a useless doctor and he'd had enough.'

'Do I need to worry?'

'Maybe. I'm really not sure. I don't think he's suicidal or anything, he mumbled something about breakfast, but he's been on all night and I don't think it was pretty. I don't know, Samira will tell you more, she's still here but she's on her way out so you'll need to catch her quick.'

'OK.'

He found her in the kitchen, and she told him about the delivery Patrick had helped with. 'He dithered a bit, but in the end he got the ventouse on and lifted the baby out at the second attempt and it's fine, it's been checked and it's all good. The mum had a second degree tear, but I was expecting that, and I repaired it because he was blaming himself, but there was nobody else available and he did well. I haven't done my ventouse training yet, and he said he'd only done it once under supervision with you, but it was madness all night, just like the day had been, so there wasn't really a choice, but he was a mess by the end of it.'

'OK. Thanks. I'll ring him.'

Patrick didn't answer, but for some reason, probably because it was saving it all for later, the unit was quiet, so after a quick word to his first pre-op patient Matt headed out to the Park Café. It was Patrick's favourite haunt according to Sally, and he found him there, slumped over a coffee with a croissant shredded into a million bits on the table in front of him.

'Hey,' he said softly, and Patrick raised his

head and looked him in the eye for a second before returning his attention to the croissant, pushing the flakes around on the table, arranging them into little rows.

He put his hand over Patrick's to stop him, and he looked up again.

'Talk to me,' he said, and Patrick shrugged.

'There's nothing to say. I can't do it any more, Mr Blake. I'm no good, and I'm never going to be any good.'

'I disagree. You're a good doctor, but you lack confidence and that'll come with experience. We all go through it. I haven't forgotten what it's like to be in your shoes. It can be terrifying, I realise that. Even now there are days when I think I have no idea what the best course of action is, but that's when you fall back on your training, your experience and your intuition. And it won't always work. Sometimes we lose.'

'Yeah, but—babies? I so nearly screwed up last night, and a baby could have died.'

'That's not what I heard. I've spoken to Samira, she said you did well, and the mother and baby are doing fine.'

'But she tore, and the baby's head was really distorted—'

'Stop it. Right there. By the time you were

needed, she'd been pushing for two hours, and the baby's head would have moulded to her pelvis.'

'But it was wonky.'

'They often are, especially if they're large, which is why she tore, not because of what you did. And yes, the suction cup will leave a mark, and it might leave a swelling, but you did it, the baby's fine, the mother is fine. Samira stitched her, she's all good, a paediatrician has looked at the baby and is satisfied that it's unharmed—you did a good job, Patrick, and if you hadn't been there, the baby might well have died, so stop beating yourself up over it. Go home, get some rest, and when you come back I want you with me as much as possible. I'll coach you through this rotation. I'm not going to let you give up. OK?'

He swallowed, then nodded. 'OK. But I still don't think I'm cut out for it.'

'Maybe not obstetrics, and maybe not hospital medicine, but if you go into general practice the body of knowledge you've acquired here will be very useful.'

Patrick nodded, and Dan had to hope he believed him, but he was out of time.

'Look, I have to go now, but I'm here for you, OK? You've got my number. Talk to me,

Patrick, that's what I'm here for. You're not alone,' he said, and with a pat on his shoulder he left him to it.

The day had been long, complicated and challenging with very few breaks, and by the end of it the only thing that was keeping her going was adrenaline.

She'd spent the last three hours with a woman who'd had to leave her husband with their three other children. She was coping alone and doing really well up to now, but the baby was overdue, it was five years since the last, and she'd had a long second stage. And now, just to add to the list, the baby was wedged in her pelvis, one shoulder jammed over her pubic bone, and when Georgie rang for help Patrick appeared.

Not the midwife she was hoping for, and there were none available because of course everyone had decided to deliver at once and they were all busy, but he looked edgy and unhappy and she'd heard about his meltdown. He was the last person she needed on this because if it didn't work seamlessly the child would be left with damage to the brachial plexus or worse. And time was of the essence.

'Is Jo around?' she asked, and he shook his head.

'She's in Theatre. I think Mr Blake's still here, he was a minute ago. Do you want me to check?'

She felt a rush of relief. 'Absolutely. Tell him it's a shoulder dystocia, and if he's not about, then find someone else. Quick as you can.'

He nodded and ran, leaving her alone with a distressed woman and no way of delivering her without skilled assistance, and she had five minutes to resolve this before it all went pear-shaped.

'OK, Vicky, let's roll you onto all fours and see if that takes the pressure off,' she suggested, and she'd just got her into position and checked the baby's heartbeat when she heard the door open and close and the snap of gloves going on.

Please, please let it be Dan—

'What have you tried?' he said quietly from behind her, and she could have cried with relief.

'Nothing yet, just turned her over. The anterior shoulder's wedged over the pubic bone and my fingers aren't long enough or strong enough to shift it, but the baby's heartbeat is OK at the moment. You've got about a minute before she has another contraction,' she added quietly, and he nodded and laid a gentle hand on the woman's back.

'Hi there, Vicky, I'm Daniel Blake, one of the consultants, and this is Dr Green. He's going to be assisting me.'

He'd brought Patrick with him? Georgie turned, gave him a reassuring smile, and turned back to Vicky.

'OK, Vicky,' Dan said, his voice all confident reassurance. 'Let's see if we can get your baby into a better position. It may not be very comfortable, I'm afraid.'

'I don't care, do whatever it takes to get it out, please,' she sobbed, and he squirted lubricant on his fingers while Georgie rubbed her back to soothe her and to try and ease the strain.

'OK. I'm going to see if I can coax this shoulder round gently, Vicky, so you'll feel a bit of pushing and shoving. Just brace against me, if you can.'

Giving a running commentary, mostly she suspected for Patrick's benefit, Dan eased his fingers in under the baby's head, frowned, pushed the head back firmly with the other hand and she saw his forearm tense and then the frown went and he eased the pressure off the baby's head just as another contraction started.

'Perfect,' he murmured as the baby's head crowned, and he stepped back with a smile and glanced at Georgie. 'Yours, I think,' he said, and stood back and watched as she took over again and finished the delivery. She almost sagged with relief as the baby was born safe and sound with both arms waving.

'Time of birth: twenty-twenty-six. Shoulder looks good,' he said, and she lay the wailing little boy down and helped Vicky turn over, then laid him on her chest. He was rooting, and with the deft hands of experience Vicky shifted him into position and he started to suckle immediately.

'Goodness, he's a big boy,' she said, and her face was all tears and smiles, the pain forgotten. 'Hello, trouble,' she murmured softly, stroking him with infinite tenderness. 'Your daddy's going to be so proud of you.'

She glanced up at them, tears welling. 'Thank you so much, both of you. I really thought...'

'Shh,' Georgie said, and gave her a little hug. 'You did really well. I expect his daddy will be proud of *you*, never mind your son. You were a star. Well, and Mr Blake. I expect he deserves a little credit for it,' she teased, and he gave a soft chuckle.

'You're too kind. Apgar nine at one minute,' he added, and wrote it in the notes, just as Kat appeared.

'Sorry, Georgie, it's been manic. Anything I can do?'

'Yes, you can relieve Mr Blake and Dr Green.'

Dan chipped in. 'Actually, Kat, you could find another midwife and relieve Georgie, too. She should have finished at seven. And page the paediatrician on call. It was a shoulder dystocia but it's looking good, just needs a check.'

Kat smiled. 'Sure. I'll page Paeds and go and get Samira, she's just finishing up some notes. See you in a minute.'

'You don't need to—'

'Yes, I do, and we're free now and you've done the best bit,' Kat said with a wink.

Vicky reached out and took her hand. 'She's right, Georgie. You look exhausted, love. You go home to bed. I'll be fine with her. As she said, you've done the best bit and you were brilliant. I can't thank you enough.'

'My pleasure, Vicky. It's what I'm here for. I'll come and see you tomorrow before you go home, if I can. And in the meantime, let's take some pictures of you to send to your husband.'

She heard Dan talking quietly to Patrick, and the moment Kat came back they left, probably to debrief.

'Right, where are we up to?' Kat asked, all smiles and business, and Georgie gave a quiet sigh of relief and filled her in on the details.

* * *

It was almost nine by the time she'd done the handover and changed, and to her surprise Dan was still there, leaning on the wall in the stairwell with his phone in his hand when she left the ward.

'Don't tell me you waited for me?' she said, feeling a pang of guilt, but he smiled and pressed the lift button.

'No, but I was about to message you, I thought you might want a lift if you hadn't already gone.'

'You've got the car?'

He nodded, and she could have cried with relief. 'I can't believe that. How come?'

'I left early because I had a difficult case first thing and I wanted to make sure I was ready. Plus I knew you were doing a twelve-hour shift that was likely to run over.'

'Oh, Dan, you are such a star. I know I don't live far away, but I am utterly shattered today. I feel as if I could sleep for a week.' She leant against the wall of the lift and met his eyes. 'Thanks again for rescuing me with Vicky.'

'My pleasure. I've been talking through the shoulder dystocia with Patrick, giving him a bit of mentoring and moral support.'

'I heard about his meltdown,' she said, and he rolled his eyes.

'I think everybody has, but I think I've talked him down off the precipice. He'll be OK.'

The lift doors opened and they walked out into the cool of the evening. It was dark, with only the lights of the car park to guide them, and he led her to his car, opened the door for her and she sank into the soft leather seat and sighed with relief.

'Have you got anything to eat at home?' he asked, and she shook her head.

'No, but I don't care. I'm too tired to eat. I'll have a bit of toast.'

'No you won't, you'll have something proper. I did a batch cook last night for you and it's in my fridge. We'll go to mine.'

She couldn't be bothered to argue. She'd eaten nothing but ginger biscuits all day, and she knew if her blood sugar got much lower she'd start to feel sick again, so she gave in without a fight, rested her head back and was almost asleep by the time they pulled up on his drive.

'Cottage pie or chicken and mushroom risotto?' he asked as they went in, and she shrugged, the effort of making a decision almost too much for her.

'Risotto?' she said, not really caring either way because she was starting to feel queasy, and he nodded, wheeled her to the sofa, sat her down and came back six minutes later with a steaming bowl.

'Where's yours?'

'In the microwave. Start without me, I'll be back in a second.'

She tasted it cautiously, then spread it out a bit, picking at the edges until it cooled enough to eat, because it was delicious and she was ready to inhale it.

'Is that OK?' he asked, coming back and sitting down beside her on the sofa.

'Yes, it's lovely, it's just a bit hot.' She turned her head and smiled at him. 'Thank you.'

'What for?'

She shrugged. 'The food, the lift, rescuing Vicky in time. If you'd gone home...'

'You would have found a way.'

She shook her head. 'I don't think so and I nearly had a fit when Patrick walked in because I don't think he would have been deft enough to do it. That kind of controlled force needs to be applied with skill or you can do so much damage, and it would have completely freaked him out. I'd already had a feel and I could barely reach. I couldn't get up over that shoulder far enough to do any good, and I don't think I would have been strong enough anyway.' She summoned the energy to smile. 'It galls me to say it, but I needed your carefully controlled brute force again,' she added, and he chuckled.

'You're welcome—but you could always say skill and experience,' he said ruefully, and she grinned at him.

'That too, then, if you insist,' she said with a little wink.

He gave another chuckle, and then leant over and dropped a kiss on her cheek that made her skin tingle and her heart do something weird.

'That's more like it. Eat up.'

She ate every last scrap, but by the time he'd taken their plates away through to the kitchen and come back with a cup of ginger and lemon tea for her, she was asleep.

He wasn't surprised. She'd dozed off in the car on a five-minute journey, and he had no idea how she'd kept going. She'd looked exhausted when he'd gone into Vicky's room, and that was well over an hour ago.

He sat down beside her and stroked her cheek with his fingers, but she didn't react and he didn't have the heart to wake her. He wasn't even sure he could, but the sofa wasn't long enough for her to stretch out on properly, and the spare bed was covered in clean laundry waiting to be folded or ironed. And anyway, it wasn't made because he didn't even know where the spare bedding was, he hadn't got that far with the unpacking.

That left only one option, and he wasn't sure what she'd think of it.

He ran upstairs, turned back his duvet, went back down and scooped her gently up in his arms and carried her up to bed.

She sighed and rolled over as he laid her down, and he eased off her shoes, covered her with the duvet and left the door open while he went downstairs to tidy up and get some fresh water in case she wanted a drink in the night.

By the time he got back she was snoring softly, and he smiled, undressed down to his shorts and slid in beside her, leaving the door open and the bathroom light on in case she woke, because she'd never been upstairs in his house and he knew she'd be disorientated.

He lay for a while and watched her sleep, watched the slight flutter of her eyelids as she dreamed, and he wondered what she was dreaming about. Nothing scary, he didn't think, because she made a tiny, contented noise and settled again, and he closed his eyes and drifted off to sleep, oddly glad to have her beside him.

* * *

Where was she? And what was that weight on her?

She felt a moment of panic, then heard a soft snore and her eyes flew open.

She was in bed—not hers—in a bedroom with a dormer window and a sloping ceiling. Dan's room, in his house, she realised as she surfaced a little more. Why? Why was she here still, and in his bed, of all places?

The last thing she remembered was eating the food he'd given her. She must have fallen asleep, but surely he would have woken her and taken her home?

Unless he'd been too tired himself? She was absolutely certain he didn't have an ulterior motive.

Whatever, he was fast asleep now, and the weight she could feel was his arm draped over her waist, the warmth from his body close behind her.

Very close, and she needed the bathroom, because the baby was pressing on her bladder. How could she get out without disturbing him?

She circled his wrist with her hand and lifted it, then slid out from underneath it and laid it down, and he sighed and stirred slightly.

Nothing more, so she crept out onto the landing and found he'd left the bathroom door open and the light on over the mirror. So she could find it in the dark?

Maybe. She was as quiet as she could be, and while she was in there she took off her bra, sliding the straps out down the sleeves of her T-shirt, and wriggled out of her jeans, but when she crept back to the bedroom he'd moved, sprawling flat on his front all across the bed like a giant starfish. So now what? Did she wake him? Find her shoes, wherever they might be, and creep out and go home?

No. He'd worry then, and anyway his bed was warm and comfy and she was quite happy to get back into it, if she could only find a square inch to lie on.

She tried moving his arm, and he grunted, lifted his head and stared at her for a second, then sat up and scrubbed his hands through his hair.

'You OK?' he asked sleepily, and she nodded.

'I just needed the loo, but you sort of claimed the whole bed while I was gone.'

He laughed softly, lay down again and shifted right across out of reach. 'Sorry. That's years of having the bed to myself. Is that better?'

'Much.' She lay down again facing him and met his eyes, but it was too dark to read them.

She was suddenly acutely aware of him, of the fact that all there was between them was a pair of skimpy knickers and a T-shirt. Unless he had anything on? She hadn't noticed, and she certainly wasn't asking, but his chest was bare and that was bad enough.

'So how come I'm in your bed?' she asked, trying to sound casual.

His smile was a little crooked. 'You fell asleep, and I didn't have the heart to wake you, and I have no idea where the bedding is for the spare room so I did what I could. I hope that's OK?'

She found a tiny smile. 'Of course it's OK. Thank you. I'm sorry I fell asleep like that. I'm tired all the time now.'

'I'm sure you are, and yesterday was a very long day. There's a lot going on in your body. Making babies is challenging.'

'It wasn't that challenging,' she joked without engaging her brain, and then held her breath as he stared at her, their eyes locked, until a slow smile dawned on his mouth. A lazy, sexy, slightly rueful smile that made her heart turn over.

'No, it really wasn't, was it?' he murmured, his voice all smoky chocolate. He rolled to face her and their legs met and settled, and he lifted a hand and cradled her cheek, his thumb grazing softly over her lips and sending her pulse racing and her mind into orbit.

'I thought we weren't going to do this,' he said softly, his eyes still locked on hers, a question in them that she couldn't answer. Or at least not in any sensible way.

They weren't going to do it. They weren't supposed to be doing it. Doing anything other than being friends, but she wanted to. Was it wise? No. Would they? Maybe...

His thumb stroked her lips again, and she could feel the slight tug on the damp skin as she parted them, feel the hitch in her breath, the beat of her heart against her ribs.

Would they?

This was such a bad idea.

Lying there with her, their legs touching, her lips soft and warm and damp under his thumb, her eyes fixed on his, almost luminous in the half-dark of the bedroom—it was a bad idea. A beautiful, wonderful, really, really bad idea.

He wanted her. So much. If only it weren't so complicated...

He moved his hand away from those tempting lips, stroking the side of her neck in a gentle caress, and he could feel the beat of her pulse under his fingertips.

Was it so complicated? Was it, really?

She was having his baby, for heaven's sake. How much more complicated could it get? It couldn't. They were already bound by a relationship deeper than he could ever have imagined.

But it wasn't what they'd agreed, was it? Or was it?

One day at a time, they'd said, and maybe today—or tonight—was the time to make a decision.

Just—what decision?

He wrestled with it for so long that in the end she made it for him. Her eyes drifted shut, and he let out a soft huff of laughter.

'Come here,' he murmured, and gathered her gently up against his chest, rolling onto his back so she could settle her head on his shoulder.

Their legs tangled, one of hers over his, an arm draped over his chest, palm flat against the skin above his heart. He could feel the soft press of her breasts against his side, the drift of her breath across his skin as she slept, and it felt right.

Torture, but in a good way, because although he still wanted her, now wasn't the time and that was probably a good thing. He'd done enough damage already. The last thing she needed was him upsetting their fragile status quo. It had to last for the next eighteen years or more, and compromising it so soon was never going to be sensible.

He gave a quiet sigh, closed his eyes and drifted off to sleep.

She was woken, as usual, by the pressure on her bladder which was becoming a constant feature of this pregnancy.

She didn't want to move, couldn't bring herself to face the day already, but she had no choice, so she peeled her arm carefully from his chest, pushed herself up and wriggled over the mattress to her side.

A glance at the digital clock on his bedside table told her it was ten to six. She needed to go. She was due back at work at seven, and she wanted to pop in and see Vicky before it all kicked off, so she picked up her clothes and shoes, tiptoed out to the bathroom and dressed while she was in there, then crept downstairs, wincing with every creaky step.

The latch on the front door wasn't deadlocked, to her relief, and it opened smoothly. She clicked it shut behind her, walked briskly home, put some toast in the toaster, showered, dressed and ran back down, grabbing the toast on the way out.

Not the most organised start to her day, but she'd slept well, thanks to Dan. Too well, because she'd thought...

No. It wouldn't have been a good idea.

He was woken by the sound of running water, and by the agonising tingling in his arm of pins and needles. He lay and massaged it until the blood returned, heard the bathroom door open and the creak of the stairs. She must be going down to get something to eat, he thought, but then he heard the sound of the front door closing, and he sat up and realised her clothes were gone, and she'd left.

Wise. He'd woken with a raging erection and an urgent need to bang his head against the wall to knock some sense into it, and if she'd come back to bed...

As it was he was going to be late. By the time he'd had a shower, scarfed down a bowl of breakfast cereal and arrived on the labour ward, it was ten to seven.

Would he end up working with her? And would it be OK?

He had no idea, and he didn't find out for a while, because Patrick collared him for a chat about his night shift, and then he did a quick ward round of his gynae post-ops before going down to the ED to see a pregnant woman who'd been involved in a car accident.

She had a closed fracture of her wrist which needed reducing, but he was worried about the impact of the collision on her uterus and the risk of a placental abruption at thirty-three weeks, so he left instructions that as soon as her fracture was reduced she should be admitted to the antenatal ward for monitoring.

His pager went, and of course the maternity lift was busy, so he ran up the stairs two at a time and arrived at the top as Georgie emerged from the lift.

'Morning,' he said, trying to sound casual, and she smiled at him a little warily.

'Hi.'

'You OK?' he asked, not sure what he was asking exactly but needing the answer.

'Yes, I'm fine.' She looked away, glancing round to check there was nobody there. 'I'm sorry I crept out this morning but you were still asleep.'

'I wasn't, actually. I'd woken by the time you closed the door, but it was just as well because I was nearly late.'

And who knows what might have happened if she'd gone back into the room. Just as well she'd done a runner.

'I've got some news for you,' she went on. 'I've just seen Vicky off with her husband, and they've decided to call the baby Daniel George. How about that?'

He laughed, and felt the tension drain away. 'Oh, that's lovely. I feel properly chuffed by that.'

'Mmm. Good, isn't it? So what's your day got in store?'

He groaned. 'No idea, but we're on take and I've just come back from the ED, so stand by for chaos. It's funny, it's always quiet for Ben.'

'I don't think that's quite true,' she said with a chuckle, but the phone was ringing as they entered the ward and they parted company at the desk, leaving him to deal with another emergency on the way in, a woman with uncontrollable bleeding from fibroids. He took her straight to Theatre for a hysterectomy, and by lunchtime he was in Theatre doing an emergency section on the woman from the ED, but both she and the baby were fine, and his pager was blissfully quiet, so he headed for the Park Café and found Georgie there with another woman.

That was unfortunate. He'd wanted to talk to her, but that wasn't going to happen now. He wondered who the other woman was. He didn't recognise her, but maybe it was just as well that she was there. It might stop him saying anything stupid. He slapped on a smile and went over to them.

A shadow fell over their table, and she looked up and her heart did a little jig.

Stupid. So stupid—

'Dan, hi,' she said, really glad that Laura was there with her because all she could think about was last night. 'Have you met Laura Stryker?'

'No, I haven't. It's good to meet you.'

'And you,' Laura said. 'How's the cottage? Any issues?'

'No, none at all, I love it. Look, I need to grab some lunch. Can I get either of you anything?'

'No, I'm fine, I need to get back to the ED,' Laura said, getting to her feet. 'Good to meet you, Dan.'

'And you. It's good to put a face to the name.'

Laura walked away, and Dan looked down at Georgie, his eyes unreadable with the light behind him.

'So, do you need anything?'

Apart from her head examined? 'I wouldn't mind an apple turnover,' she said, and he nodded and walked off, heading to the café entrance. She stared after him, wondering where they'd go from here.

Back to bed to finish what they'd very nearly started? Or back to square one of being friends and steadfastly ignoring whatever it was that wanted to pull them together?

She had no idea, and she wasn't sure Dan did, either, so when he came back she raised the subject.

'I've been thinking. If I hadn't been pregnant, I wouldn't have been with you last night, would I?'

He met her eyes, then looked away. 'No. Probably not.'

'So, it really isn't a good idea letting it happen again. We so nearly…'

'Yeah. We did.'

'And if I wasn't pregnant, we wouldn't have been in that situation, so why put ourselves in it now? It's so early, Dan. I could lose this baby so easily, lots of people do, and then where would we be? Together, for what? Random sex with someone we work with? That's never a good idea. And I really don't feel ready for anything else, and I'm not sure you are.'

He nodded slowly. 'No. You're right, I'm not sure I'll ever be ready—which doesn't mean I don't like you, because I do, a lot, and if it wasn't for Holly and the baby then maybe I'd feel differently about us, but you're right, it's very early, and if all goes well with the baby we've got plenty of time to think about this. Who knows?'

He glanced back at her, and she smiled at him.

'Yup. I guess we could be in and out of each other's lives for twenty years or more.'

'Or more than that. Graduations, weddings, grandchildren.'

'Grandchildren?' She started to laugh, and he gave a rueful grin and shrugged his shoulders.

'Just a natural progression of thoughts. Can I drop round tonight? I've got those meals for you. I put them in the freezer last night, so they're all ready to go.'

'That would be lovely. Thank you—'

'Oh, for goodness' sake!' He pulled his pager out, glared at it and rolled his eyes. 'Sorry, I've got to go. I'm needed on Gynae.'

He looked at his sandwich and slapped his head, and she laughed. 'Go. I'll put it in the fridge for you in the labour ward. Come and get it when you can.'

'You're a star,' he said, and apparently without thinking he bent and dropped a kiss on her mouth and walked away, leaving her lips tingling.

So much for their conversation. All she could see was Dan with grey threaded through his dark hair, bouncing a grandchild on his knee, and she felt a huge knot of emotion swelling in her chest and threatening to choke her.

No. It was way too soon to think about stuff like that. She picked up their food and headed back to work before she totally lost the plot.

CHAPTER SEVEN

HE SHOULDN'T HAVE kissed her.

He hadn't given it a nanosecond's thought, just swooped in and did what came naturally—and that was worrying.

It worried him all the rest of the day, and it was still worrying him when he arrived at Georgie's house a little after seven-thirty with the meals.

He rang the bell, and when she answered the door he held out the carrier bag and she took it and peered inside.

'Gosh, that looks lovely. Thank you so much. Are you coming in?'

He shook his head. 'No, I'll go home and cook for myself now. I'm hungry.'

'Or you could eat with me?' she suggested, and he wasn't sure if she was being polite or really meant it.

'Are you sure?' he asked, and she laughed and walked off into the kitchen. He heard the whirr of the microwave starting up as he stepped into the hall and closed the door, and she turned and smiled at him as he leant against the kitchen doorway and folded his arms.

'I should apologise about last night. I didn't mean to stir things up,' he said, and her smile softened.

'Nothing happened last night,' she reminded him gently. 'You were a perfect gentleman, and you looked after me. That's all, Dan. All it needs to be.'

What about what I want it to be?

Not that that mattered. That was just his body talking, and she obviously didn't want the same thing, if he even knew what that was. He nodded slowly, the fight between his head, his heart and his body too confusing to deal with right now, and their earlier conversation had done nothing to clarify it, at least for his body and possibly his confused and relentlessly optimistic heart. 'OK. I just didn't want you not to feel comfortable with me.'

She laughed at that, but her eyes were gentle and he wanted nothing more than to pull her into his arms and hold her. 'Daniel Blake, you really aren't very observant. I slept like a log. Would I do that if I wasn't comfortable with you?'

He smiled and nodded again. 'OK. I'll give you that. So what are we having?'

'Cottage pie. I thought I'd ring the changes. What do you want with it? Tenderstem broccoli, or some sugar snap peas, or baby carrots, or—ooh, what's this?'

'Ruby chard. You can slice it up and steam it in the microwave for a minute or two like spinach. It's out of the garden.'

'Really? Wow. Let's try that, then,' she said with a smile, and he took it off her, washed it, sliced it and piled it in a lidded dish while she checked the cottage pies.

'Ouch. They're done,' she said, licking the finger she'd stuck in one, and he rolled his eyes and put the chard into the empty microwave.

And then he turned and bumped into her, and their eyes clashed and he stepped away with a hasty apology and a whole host of regrets.

Some for coming in instead of going home again, but mostly for not having followed through last night.

He didn't stay long that evening, and after that they settled into a kind of routine.

He made some more meals for her, simple but tasty things which she would never have been able to cook but managed to eat, like a pea and mushroom risotto, a rich chicken casserole with mushrooms, prunes and apricots for the iron, more of the cottage pies— and he froze them in portions and delivered them on a regular basis, complete with iron-rich fresh vegetables like broccoli, asparagus, peas and spinach, and sometimes more of the ruby chard out of the garden.

He'd certainly done his research, and she was hugely grateful.

They argued about who was paying for the food, and he finally shut up and gave in. Except when they ate together at his, and then he wouldn't hear of it, and he always drove her home afterwards. No more falling asleep on his sofa, and they didn't mention it again.

Sometimes he ate at hers, sometimes she went to his, sometimes she ate alone, and gradually the weeks went by.

And then he started nagging again.

'You need to see a midwife.' 'Have you made an appointment with your GP?' 'When are you going to start accessing antenatal care?'

So she gave up when she hit the ten-week mark in the middle of October, and went to see Lucy Gallagher, her GP.

Lucy checked her over, gave her a clean bill

of health and then added, 'It's time to book you in for a scan, but you know all that.'

She did, and of course it meant a referral to the hospital.

Her hospital. Her department. Her friends.

So what now?

She left the surgery and walked straight to Dan's house. She knew he'd had the afternoon off, and conveniently she found him in the front garden digging out weeds round the edge of the drive.

He straightened up, winced and smiled at her.

'Hello, you. How are you doing?'

'OK. You look as if you've done enough for one day.'

His grin was rueful. 'Yes, you're probably right. So what's up?'

'I've just been to my GP.'

He held her eyes for a long moment, then nodded, dusted off his hands, threw the trowel into the weed bucket and led her through the side gate into the garden, locking it behind him.

'So is there a problem?' he asked, and she could see the concern in his eyes. She shook her head.

'No—well, not a medical problem, but she's referring me for a scan, so that'll open a whole can of worms any minute now. They're all going to know.'

He nodded slowly. 'OK. Have you eaten?'

She shook her head. 'No. My appointment was at five-thirty.'

'Right. Go and sit down, and I'll stick a couple of meals in the microwave now and we can talk about it.'

Not that there was much to talk about, apart from exactly how much they were going to reveal about their relationship, and who to tell first, because that would be the starting point to kick it all off.

The microwave pinged, and she joined him at the table, picking up her fork and poking her food for a moment. Too hot to eat yet, so she launched in.

'I think I need to talk to Ben before he gets the referral,' she said, and he winced and then nodded.

'Yes, of course you do. Are you going to tell him it's mine?'

She chuckled at that. 'I don't have a choice. He and Daisy are well aware I don't have a social life that involves dating, and they know about Mark, so they'll know this pregnancy is nothing short of a miracle. They will ask whose it is, though, and I will have to tell them.'

'You really think they'll ask?'

'Absolutely, and I can't say it's no one they've met, because although that's true of Daisy, it's certainly not true of Ben, and knowing him he'll work it out in seconds anyway. The fact that my conception date coincides exactly with your arrival is a bit of a giveaway. And then there's the sonographer, and the antenatal clinic reception staff who all know me from the clinics, and all the other midwives— it'll be round the hospital in minutes. And anyway, it'll soon be obvious because my clothes are already tight, but that could be your fault with all the tasty food you keep plying me with.'

'I'll take that as a compliment,' he said, then searched her eyes.

'Do you mind if they know it's me?'

She shrugged. 'No. I thought you might.'

'I don't mind, and it'll cut down all the idle speculation, but I do wonder if we ought to go public about our relationship before the scan thing comes up. Just so it's not totally out of the blue.'

She stared at him, surprised by that. 'What relationship? We're friends, that's all. Aren't we?'

His smile was wry, a little strained. 'I don't

know. It's a bit more complicated than that, really, isn't it?'

She sighed and dropped her face in her hands. 'Oh, they're all going to be talking about us,' she groaned, and she heard him chuckle.

'You could always go somewhere else.'

Her head snapped up and she stared at him in astonishment. 'Are you serious? I trust these guys! I've worked here for four years, they know me—why would I want anyone else looking after me?'

'It wasn't a serious suggestion,' he said soothingly, and then added with a wry smile, 'although I have to say if we wanted to keep it quiet the idea has some merit.'

She sighed again. 'They'll all think we're together, won't they?'

'We are together.'

'Not like that. Well, only the once.' Although it had nearly been twice, and it wouldn't have stopped at that.

He hesitated, then said very quietly, 'Maybe we should be.'

If he'd shouted the words, they wouldn't have had more impact. She felt her jaw sag, and clamped her mouth shut.

He was looking at her, his eyes deadly serious, and she felt her heart lurch and start to race. Surely he didn't mean that? No, of course not. But—what, then?

'No,' she said slowly. 'We've talked about this and I don't think we should. Not really— not properly.' Because it was only for the baby, and that wasn't a good enough reason, however tempting, and after Mark she was too wary to dare to trust her own judgement.

He shrugged and looked away. 'Just an idea. Don't dismiss it without thinking about it.'

She couldn't think about anything else.

All that night it churned over in her mind, and she woke exhausted, sick and dreading the day. She forced down some toast, promptly lost it and walked to work on legs like rubber.

She needed to find Ben, but it wasn't hard.

He was just leaving the desk when she went in, and he smiled at her, then paused and gave her a thoughtful look. 'Are you OK? You look really pale.'

'I'm fine. Can we talk?'

He searched her eyes, found something there and laid a hand gently on her shoulder. 'Sure. Come with me,' he said, and ushered her into his office. 'So what's up?'

She shook her head, and he steered her to a chair, sat her down and perched on the edge of his desk.

'Georgie, talk to me,' he said gently. 'What's wrong?'

'Nothing's wrong,' she said. 'I just feel a bit rough today.' She made herself meet his eyes, and found nothing but concern. 'I'm pregnant.'

He stared at her for a moment, then gave a low chuckle. 'Well, you dark horse,' he said, and hugged her gently. 'That's amazing. Congratulations. I take it we *are* celebrating?'

She tried to smile, but then her eyes welled and she shrugged. 'I don't know, Ben. I don't honestly know how I feel. Shocked, overjoyed, confused?'

'Not planned, then?'

That startled a laugh out of her. 'How could it possibly be planned? You know perfectly well I've had fertility issues. I didn't imagine for a moment this could happen.'

'Which of course is how it did,' he said slowly, and then added, 'Does Dan know yet?'

She stared at him, not surprised, just... 'How on earth?'

'Are you kidding? I'm no stranger to chemistry, Georgie, and you guys have it in spades. So, does he know, or are we going to have to keep this under wraps?'

'Keep it under wraps?' She laughed out loud. 'Ben, I'm pregnant. With the best will in the world, we can't keep it under wraps—but yes, he knows. He's known for weeks.'

'So how many weeks are you?'

'Ten.'

His eyes widened. 'Ten?'

She sighed and rolled her eyes. 'Yes. Ten. And before you get a calculator out, it was his first day.'

Ben's mouth opened, shut again and he stifled a smile. 'Like I said, chemistry. So have you seen anyone yet?'

'My GP—Lucy Gallagher. She's referring me for a scan, so I'm just telling you before you find out.'

'OK. Well, it's safe with me. Are you going to tell anyone else yet?'

'Jan,' she said, wondering what her boss would make of it. 'And maybe Liv. I work with her quite often and she doesn't miss a lot.'

He nodded. 'Can I tell Daisy?'

She shook her head. 'No, let me tell her. It's… It's complicated.'

His mouth quirked. 'I can imagine. That's a pretty quick courtship.'

She felt herself colouring and looked away. 'No courtship, Ben. We're not together. Well, not like that. It was a one-off. And he's been amazing, very supportive, but—well, I'm not looking for a relationship, not after the last time. I don't think I could trust anyone again, and he has issues, too, but he is the baby's father, and he definitely wants to be involved, so we're doing this together and we're friends. That's all.'

'I'm not judging, Georgie. You're entitled to a life, and I'm glad he's being supportive. Does he know you're telling me?'

She nodded. 'Yes, he knows. He's fine with it.' As fine as he was about any of it, and in truth she didn't have a clue how fine he was with it at all.

'Good. So, who do you want to look after you? Because obviously Dan can't, which leaves Nick, Jake and Emily.'

'And you.'

'Are you OK with that?'

She smiled a little sadly. 'Not if you don't think I should be, but I don't think I could be in better hands.'

He gave her a gentle smile. 'Thank you. We'd all look after you, Georgie, but it's up to you who you choose and I won't be offended if you don't want me. You don't have to decide yet, though, there's plenty of time,' he added, and he shrugged away from the desk and pulled her to her feet and hugged her properly.

'We're here for you, you know that,' he said

gruffly. 'Me and Daisy. Anything you want or need, just ask. And I'll do my best to keep it quiet for as long as we can. And in the meantime, don't shut the door on Dan. He's a very decent human being, and you don't know what might happen between you, so never say never.'

She blinked away sudden tears and hugged him back.

'Thank you for being so understanding.'

'Don't be daft.' He let her go, gave her a stern look and told her to go and get something to eat before she fell over.

He was as good as his word.

He didn't even mention it to Dan, but he didn't need to because she gave him a heads-up over lunch. Well, lunch. A handful of ginger biscuits, her default high-carb stopgap, eaten hastily in the ward kitchen just before three, so not really lunch, and not much of an opportunity to talk, but she felt he should know she'd done it.

She told Liv, who hugged her hard and, like Ben, offered any help she needed, and she told Jan.

Jan was unshockable, and her main concern was for the health of Georgie and the baby, so she tore up the rota and took her off nights, which was kind because nights on maternity were a special kind of hell, and she even sent her home on time at the end of her shift, so she called in on Daisy on the way home and told her not to yell at Ben because she'd sworn him to secrecy.

Then Dan rang her, and she said goodbye to Daisy and went round to his house and told him everything Ben had said. Well, most of it. Not the bit about not closing the door on him. He didn't need to know Ben was matchmaking, especially when there wasn't a prayer of her letting him into her life in that way just because he felt it was the right thing to do.

And then three days later she got her scan appointment, and it all suddenly felt much more real.

The next week took for ever to pass, but finally it was time, and she met Dan down in the antenatal clinic at five-thirty, right at the end of the clinic.

'Hi, Georgie,' the sonographer said, then looked at Dan, said nothing more but welcomed them both in with a wide and slightly surprised smile.

Georgie didn't really feel like smiling. She was a mass of nerves, still not quite able to believe she could be pregnant. She lay down on the couch with Dan by her side and they watched the screen as Steph ran the transducer over her little bump.

It had been there a week already, popping up out of the constraints of her pelvis. It had been a huge relief because it was no longer squashing her bladder, but she'd been quite surprised that it had happened so soon in a first pregnancy.

The grainy image appeared, changing as Steph moved the head of the scanner over her skin, and then there it was, the image of a baby, the tiny nose clearly visible in its face, the little limbs, all present and correct, the heart beating steadily, a rapid little whoosh that they could hear quite clearly.

She felt Dan squeeze her hand, and she sucked in her breath and pressed her fingers to her mouth.

'I really am pregnant,' she said softly, and Dan laughed.

'Yes, you really are,' he said, his voice slightly choked—and then the sound changed and her breath caught. *Two* foetal heartbeats?

She listened in stunned silence, not quite sure she was hearing what she thought she was hearing, because the sound was becoming drowned out by the roar of her own heart.

'Is that an echo? Or the cord?'

Steph shook her head. 'I don't think so. There's a double whoosh. The cord's more of a thud.'

Her heart hitched, and Steph moved the head again, and she heard Dan suck in his breath as another perfect little baby came into view.

'There are two,' he murmured, and he squeezed her hand.

'Yes, there are. You've got twins in there, Georgie, and I think they're identical,' Steph said with a smile, and then she ran the transducer over the placental area and confirmed it. There was only one placenta, and Georgie's pulse ramped up a notch.

Identical twins were more prone to problems and congenital abnormalities than fraternal twins, but at least they were the same size and both the hearts were beating well, the heartbeats strong and bold, beating in unison, and she felt a sudden rush of love so powerful it took her breath away, and gradually the shock gave way to a flicker of pure, unadulterated joy.

She stared at the screen as Steph went back over the little twins, and she was overwhelmed.

'Twins? Really?' she murmured, and Steph met her eyes and smiled.

'I'll call Mr Walker. He'll want to look at this, he oversees all the twin pregnancies. He's in the clinic now.'

Dan's hand found hers in a firm, steady grip, and she clung to him as Steph made the call. Moments later there was a knock on the door and Ben came in, winked at her and studied the image frozen on the screen, then picked up the transducer.

'Right, let's have a closer look at these little guys,' he said cheerfully, and she lay there and watched as he moved around from side to side, examining every angle until he was satisfied.

'Well, they're definitely monochorionic, there's only one placenta and one chorion, so they're identical for sure.'

'What about the aminion? Are they mono-amniotic as well?' Dan asked, and Georgie's pulse hitched up a notch. Not another layer of complication…

'Too early to tell. The amnion's often hard to spot at this stage. How many weeks are you?'

'Eleven plus four.'

'OK. I think we need to scan you again in a week, but it's looking good so far and mono-chorionic monoamniotic twins are extremely rare, so it's unlikely.'

He looked at Steph. 'Can you save all these

images, please, and we'll compare them next time, and then we might go for a 3D scan and maybe 4D for greater clarity?'

She nodded, and he looked at them both and smiled.

'Any questions?'

Georgie shook her head, still numb with shock, and behind her Dan murmured something that could have been no. He sounded like she felt. Leave it to an obstetrician and a midwife to go for the unusual, she thought.

'OK. I need to get back to my clinic, but if you want to talk about it, my door's always open.'

They walked out of the clinic in a daze. At least he was, and he was pretty sure Georgie was, too, but at least they didn't have to walk home. He'd brought the car because it had been raining that morning, and he was glad he had because his legs were like jelly.

'Yours or mine?' he asked, and she shrugged.

'Yours, I think. I haven't got much food.'

He fired up the car and headed out of the car park, his mind full of the images they'd seen.

Twins? Really?

He turned onto the drive, cut the engine and opened the door, and they walked into the sitting room and sat down as if their strings were cut.

'I can't believe it,' she said, and he squeezed her hand, as much for his own comfort as hers.

'No, nor can I, but it's definitely real. I recorded their heartbeats,' he said, getting out his phone, and he pressed play and they listened.

'What are you thinking?' she said softly, and he looked up at her wary face and tried to smile.

'I think we're having two babies,' he said, and there was a catch in his voice.

She nodded. 'Is that OK?'

He laughed, but it came out more like a sob. 'Yes, it's OK. It's incredible. It's just a bit much to take in all at once.'

'Will you be able to come to the next scan?'

She was putting on a brave face but she looked a little shocked still, maybe even on the verge of tears, and apart from when she'd told him she was pregnant and he'd behaved like an ass, he'd never seen her like that.

'Of course I'll come. You know that. Come here.'

He reached for her, and she snuggled against him and let him hold her, and his mind went into hyperdrive.

Twins, for heaven's sake! How on earth had that happened? Of all the crazy things.

'Fancy a pasta bake?' he asked, and she nodded.

'Anything. I'm starving.'

'Eating for three?' he said wryly, but she just shook her head slowly, still dazed.

'How?' she asked, following him into the kitchen. 'It's like buses. You wait for ages, then two come at once.'

That made him laugh, and he put the pasta bakes into the microwave and pulled her into his arms.

'They'll be OK,' he said. 'Lots of people have twins.'

'I know, but—really?'

He was totally in agreement with that, and there was no way she'd be able to look after two babies on her own. Twins were hardcore. On top of the demands of two babies on her pregnant body, and the sheer physical effort of carrying them around all that time, there was the probability of a Caesarean section, followed by sleepless nights and the relentless task of caring for two tiny and very demanding little human beings while recovering from major surgery.

It changed everything. And she could argue all she wanted, but he was looking after her, like it or not, because this was his fault, his responsibility.

And he was going to fulfil that responsibility if it was the last thing he did.

'Move in with me,' he murmured, and she lifted her head and stared at him.

'What? Why?'

He shrugged. 'Because I don't want you to be alone? Because I want to be able to look after you without one or other of us running backwards and forwards? This is a whole different ball game, Georgie.'

She looked away.

'So what are you suggesting?' she asked, and he hesitated, because he wasn't sure.

'Honestly? I don't know. I just know that a twin pregnancy isn't a bundle of laughs, and I don't want you getting any more exhausted than you have to.'

'You don't need to look after me. I'm quite capable of looking after myself, and you're doing enough already.'

'At the moment, maybe. But maybe not enough in the long term.'

'Well, can't we deal with that if and when we get there?'

If and when? Or as and when?

'OK,' he agreed, although he didn't really agree. 'But the offer stands.'

She kissed his cheek and moved away. 'Thank you. I'll bear it in mind. Anything I can do?'

'No, you're fine, they're nearly done. Sit and talk to me.'

She did, and then after they'd eaten he cleared the table and loaded the dishwasher.

'Do you want anything else? Yogurt? A hot drink?'

She shook her head. 'No, thanks. That was lovely, but I need to go home now. I'm tired and I ache, and I could do with a bath and an early night.'

He pulled her to her feet and settled his hands on her shoulders.

'It'll be OK, Georgie,' he said, and she stared straight into his eyes.

'Will it?' she asked wryly, and he couldn't answer because there was no way he could tell, and she knew that as well as he did.

'I'll run you home,' he said, and stopped her reply with a finger against her lips. 'That's not negotiable,' he told her, softening it with a smile, and she shrugged and gave in.

The next week was agonising, and she spent much of it doing endless research into twins, mostly about monochorionic monoamniotic twins which did nothing to reassure her. But

Ben had said it was highly unlikely, and maybe the membrane wasn't visible because it had been too soon.

But by the end of the second scan, there was no doubt about it, and they could see it clearly on the screen.

Her babies were monochorionic, monoamniotic identical twins, growing inside the same amniotic sac, from the same placenta, with nothing to stop them getting entangled in each other's umbilical cords with potentially catastrophic results. And that was just the obvious. On top of that were a host of associated conditions caused by the late splitting of the embryo, and the chance of them reaching viability was slim.

And just like that, in the space of a week, her pregnancy had gone from the delightful surprise of a single baby to twins to an ultra-high-risk twin pregnancy with a very uncertain outcome.

She turned her head away, too shocked to talk, too numb to cry, the dreams she'd allowed herself to build in the past few weeks in tatters. It was left to Dan to talk to Ben, to ask Steph for photos, to ask what would happen now.

He gently wiped the gel from her skin, tugged down her scrub top and helped her up, and she stiffened her spine and followed Ben out of the room and into his consulting room, Dan at her side.

Ben was brilliant with them.

Even though they both knew all the risks and technicalities and implications for her pregnancy, he went through them meticulously, one by one, and Dan was grateful for that because his mind was in bits.

He sat by Georgie's side, her hand in his, and every now and again he could feel a shudder run through her. He shifted closer, swapped hands and put an arm around her shoulders, and she leant wordlessly against him while Ben went through it all.

How much of it she heard, he had no idea. He wasn't doing much better himself. He wanted to scream and cry and hurl things, to ask, why him? Why, after already losing one child to an obstetric complication, was he facing the threat of losing not one but two more?

MCMA was a one in ten thousand chance, and the likelihood of them surviving was slim. How cruel could life get?

'Do you want to do this later?' Ben asked gently, and Dan looked up and met his clinical lead's sympathetic eyes and shrugged.

'I don't know. Georgie?'

'I can't—I'm sorry, Ben. I can't take it in, it's just… Why me?' she asked, her voice so forlorn Dan could have cried for her.

'Hey, come on,' Ben said. 'It's not the end of the world and it could have been a lot worse. We know they aren't conjoined, which they could have been so easily, nor do they have TRAP syndrome—twin reversed arterial perfusion, where only one twin has a heart. We know that because there are definitely two hearts beating happily away.'

'What about TAPS?' she asked, which was just what Dan was thinking.

'Twin anaemia-polycythaemia syndrome means their blood vessels become linked so that one twin becomes anaemic and the other overloaded with red blood cells. It's tricky but not impossible to deal with, but it's also vanishingly rare. TTTS, twin to twin transfusion syndrome, is more likely, but again it can be dealt with. You'd be very unlucky to have either of those, so, yes, it'll be a bit tricky, but once you've reached twenty weeks you're going to have constant monitoring, very frequent scans—you'll be very closely watched throughout this.'

'Have you ever seen this before?' she asked, and he nodded.

'Yes. Yes, I have. Ten years ago we had a patient with it.'

'And?'

He smiled. 'Daisy and I delivered them the night before our wedding, and the girls are at the same school as our children, and they are both absolutely fine. So are Matt and I, and we're MCMA twins, which is pretty much why we both ended up in obstetrics and why he's a twin specialist heading up a referral unit in London. So I have a considerable personal interest in the condition, and a specialist on tap who can't tell me to get lost because I'd never speak to him again. Don't worry, we've got this. We just need to get you through the next twelve weeks, until the babies are viable. If we can do that, then we're well on the way to home and dry.'

CHAPTER EIGHT

HOME AND DRY.

Would her babies *ever* be home? Home with her, back in her little house…

Her too-little house. She'd have to move. She'd need a proper garden, especially if they were boys—if they survived that long.

She could feel the panic rising, the fear she might lose them, the fear of all that could happen to them, the possibility that they would survive against all the odds seeming so remote that she struggled to believe in it.

The doorbell rang, and she stood there, frozen. Who could it be? She didn't care, she didn't want to speak to anyone. She couldn't.

But it rang again, and then she heard knocking, and a voice through the letter box.

'Hello? Georgie? Let me in.'

Daisy. It was Daisy, and she'd never been so glad to see anyone in her life.

She opened the door and Daisy walked in, put her arms round her and hugged her hard.

'Ben told me he'd sent you home, said you might need someone to talk to that wasn't Dan. Are you OK?'

'No. I can't do this,' she mumbled into Daisy's shoulder, and Daisy tutted and led her into the sitting room, sat her down and made them both a cup of mint tea, then gave her a mock stern look.

'Right. We'll have less of that "I can't do this" nonsense,' she said candidly. 'What happened to our Georgie?'

'I'm just scared for them, Daisy. And it's weeks and weeks until they're even remotely viable. What if something happens? What if the cords get tangled before then? They'll both die and it's just so unfair. And it's not just the cord entanglement. It's all the vascular and cardiac problems—there are so many things that could go wrong that are totally out of my control. They're my *babies*, Daisy, and I can't help them, and I feel so *useless*.'

'You're not useless, and you're not alone. You've got me on tap, you've got Dan, and you've got Ben and Matt. There's no way Ben's going to let anything happen to you if he can possibly avoid it, and his brother's the godfather of twin pregnancy. You couldn't be in safer hands. Now drink your tea. And have you got any biscuits? I'm starving.'

'Only ginger.'

'They'll do. I've had a few million of them over all my pregnancies. It'll bring back fond memories.'

It was a hideous day.

He'd taken an hour out in the morning which had meant leaving his registrar in charge, but he was straight back in with a prolapsed cord needing a crash section, followed by another section with a baby in fetal distress due to a prolonged obstructed labour.

And then to put the cherry on top there was another placenta previa for his hot button. This time, however, she had notes, a booked elective section for the following day and she was already in under observation when she started contracting, so it was a simple case of taking her straight to Theatre and delivering her baby safe and sound.

Just as well, as his head was all over the place after the bombshell of the scan, and all he wanted to do was get back to Georgie and see if she was all right.

He wasn't sure he was. He'd spent the last week telling her it would be fine, they had to wait, it was too early to see the membrane, but his optimism had just taken a crashing dive and he was struggling. It was too much to take on board in the middle of a working day, too much information to process on a vanishingly rare condition that until last week had been a theoretical thing that he'd learned about in college and never expected to see in practice, and now, after the second scan, he felt out of his depth and overwhelmed by the enormity of it all.

How Georgie was doing was anybody's guess, but one thing he knew. From now on she was staying with him and he was looking after her, because there was no way either she or another baby of his were going to die if he had the slightest chance of saving them.

Always assuming she'd agree to his suggestion, and he was pretty damn sure she wouldn't.

She was about to water the garden when the doorbell rang.

Dan, inevitably. She wasn't sure she wanted to see him. He'd be bound to make a fuss, and she just felt exhausted and emotionally wrung out.

She opened the door, and he was standing there with the car outside. Odd, he almost always walked and it was fine this evening.

'May I come in?'

'If you don't fuss over me.'

He looked at her for a moment, then gave a quiet chuckle. 'How did I know you'd say that?'

He stepped inside, closing the door behind him, and gave her a gentle hug. She could have stayed there indefinitely, propped up by his strong, firm body, wrapped in the warmth of his arms, but he dropped them and let her go. 'Can we talk?'

She felt her shoulders droop. 'Do we have to? I'm so tired, Dan. It's been a hellish day. I just want to go to bed.'

'Ditto. But I have a suggestion. Well, two, really. I don't want you on your own, Georgia, not now we know what's going on, so I'd like you to come back to mine, or if you won't do that, then let me stay here, so I'm here for you.'

Why? What did he know that she didn't? She searched his eyes. 'Why?' she asked, and his eyes changed from concern to anguish.

'Because I need to look after you. I have to. I can't face losing anyone else to an obstetric complication,' he said with brutal honesty.

Oh, Dan. She'd somehow lost sight of the fact that she wasn't the only one struggling. This was the last thing he needed with his history, and for the first time that day she stopped worrying about the babies and switched her attention to him.

'Dan, I'm fine,' she said gently. 'And at the moment, the babies are fine, and even if they weren't, there's nothing you can do about it. Nothing either of us can do about it. We're in the lap of the gods.'

He looked down at her and nodded slowly. 'I know. I still won't rest if I haven't done everything that I *can* do.'

He glanced past her, and saw the watering can in the kitchen sink. 'Like that, for instance. Why are you doing that? Watering the plants with that heavy can? And anyway it's the end of October. Why do they need watering? It rained yesterday.'

'But not enough for the pots. It's not heavy, I only half fill it, and it's only for the evergreen shrubs, the rest are fine. For heaven's sake, Dan, I'm not an invalid! And watering the plants won't hurt the babies.'

He walked past her, topped the can up to the brim, picked it up and carried it out. 'Right, which ones?' he asked, and watered them while she folded her arms and watched, resisting the urge to tap her foot on the floor.

'Dan, I'm OK. I'm feeling a lot better, I've had Daisy here and she's been amazing. She made me lunch, talked sense into me and she's just round the corner if I need anything.'

'She's also got four children and can't drop everything and come, nor can she be here in the night in case you have a problem, nor can she do the little things like make you a cup of tea every time you want one—'

'I can make my own tea! I'm not an invalid!'

'Good. I'm very, very glad to hear it. But you *are* tired, you *are* pregnant with twins, and you're still working. Cut yourself some slack, Georgie, and let me help you, please.'

Light dawned. 'Is that why the car's here? So you can drive me and all my things back to yours so you can hothouse me until they're born?'

He studied her, and gave a little huff of not quite laughter. 'No. Well, maybe, but I was pretty sure you'd refuse, at least for now.'

'So—why the car? Oh, of course. It's got *your* things in.'

He sighed and looked away. 'I just want to look after you. Indulge me, for God's sake. How hard is it?'

Actually in the end it wasn't hard at all, and it was almost a relief to know she wasn't on her own. Just in case…

But they weren't having a repeat of the situation they'd had before, where she'd ended up in his bed. Far too dangerous. She handed him bedlinen, put a towel in the bathroom for him and went to bed, shutting the door firmly behind herself and leaving him to it.

She heard him pottering around in the kitchen, but it wasn't long before he came upstairs. She heard the flush of the loo, the sound of running water, then a few minutes later the click of his bedroom light switch.

Her retreat would have been more effective, she thought wryly, if she'd remembered to get herself a glass of water first so she didn't have to creep out after he'd gone quiet, but the stairs creaked under her feet, and moments later he came down and joined her in the kitchen.

'Are you OK?'

'Yes, of course I am. I'm just thirsty.'

He grinned ruefully. 'Ditto. I meant to take a glass of water up with me and forgot.' He sighed and leant against the door frame, his eyes trained on her so that she was acutely conscious of the scanty nightdress that ended somewhere well above her knees. It didn't help that it was covered in tiny cats, either. What kind of a look was that? Not that it mattered in the slightest—

'Cute cats,' he murmured, and she turned to look at him. He was wearing a tired old T-shirt with a faded, peeling picture of Superman on the front, for heaven's sake—but with snug jersey shorts that sent her pulse into hyperdrive, and he had a lazy smile on his face that made her heart hitch.

She raised an eyebrow. 'You can talk. Superman, really? How old are you?' she teased, trying to ignore the shorts, and his mouth twitched.

'It was a present from my sister years ago—and anyway, it's comfy.'

'Well, it had to have one redeeming feature,' she said with a stifled smile, and dragged her eyes off him.

She ran the tap till it was cold, handed him a glass of water and headed back upstairs, acutely conscious of him behind her. He'd have a great view straight up her skirt. She tugged the back of her nightie down a bit and kicked herself for not putting on a different one tonight. A long one. Ankle length would be good.

He followed her up without a word, hesitated in his bedroom doorway then set the glass down.

'Wait.'

She sighed and turned back. 'Now what?'

'Don't close your door. Please?'

'What?'

He gave a short, frustrated sigh and scrubbed

his hand through his hair, leaving it rumpled and sexier than ever. 'Look—I don't want to invade your space, Georgie, and I know you don't want me here, but I need to know that you're safe. If anything happened to you—'

She wrapped her arms around herself. 'You're making me nervous now. Did Ben tell you something he didn't tell me?'

'No! No, absolutely not. It's just...'

'...what happened...' she finished gently, and he nodded.

'Yes. And I can't just switch that off. It's there all the time, every day at work, every night if I have a case I'm concerned about, because I know what it means when someone dies because you haven't done enough. I've been there, and I don't want to go there again. And if that means I'm doing too much, I'm sorry, but I need to take care of you and keep you and the babies safe, and also give you the reassurance that if something does happen, you're not alone. I couldn't bear you to be alone.'

She felt her eyes fill. 'Oh, Dan. Come here,' she said softly, and pulled him gently into her arms and hugged him.

It was a mistake. Of course it was a mistake, because despite all that had happened, despite the fear and the threat to her pregnancy and his endless hovering, beneath it all was a longing to hold him, to be held by him again.

He rested his head against hers and sighed, and she felt some of the tension go out of him. His warmth seeped into her, calming the fear she was trying so hard not to acknowledge, and gradually she relaxed. But not completely.

She let him go, took a step back and smiled. 'Thank you,' she said softly, and then stepping back, she pushed the door to, leaving it open a crack, and climbed into bed. The bed where he'd held her in his arms and made love to her. The bed where they'd made their babies.

She wished she could trust him with her heart, and under any other circumstances she might well have done, but she knew he didn't want a relationship any more than she did. He wasn't just doing this because of her, he was doing it because of the babies too, because of his guilt and his fear for their safety.

And in a way she was glad he was here, because underneath her bravado and protests lay a deep well of fear and dread over what the next few weeks and months would bring. That was the reason, and the only reason, she'd let him stay.

It was no kind of a foundation for their relationship, but it was all she could have from him, all he had to offer and all she would accept, and she couldn't let herself forget that.

He stayed for the rest of that week, and by the end of it she was struggling with the forced proximity. She thought he was, too, but probably not for the same reasons. She had a feeling he felt unwelcome, and she felt crowded, hovered over, watched, even when he wasn't. And under it all was the tug of attraction that was driving her crazy.

And his sleep gear didn't help. Why did he have to be so ridiculously well put together? The odd carbuncle or bad breath or a disgusting habit would go a long way towards making it easier.

So she told him it wasn't working for her, and instead of agreeing that it was overkill anyway, he came back with another idea.

'Why don't you come back to mine?' he suggested. 'There's more space there, and I've sorted out the spare room. Or we could alternate? Stay here if we're working late, or at mine if not? And you can spend the days here when you're off duty and I'm on call, so you're nearer the hospital. How about that?'

It seemed a reasonable compromise, and she was surprised to find she actually liked the idea, so they tried it and found it worked. And every day at work he got out his Doppler and they listened to the babies' heartbeats.

So far, so good, and she started to relax. She even allowed herself to feel happy.

And then three weeks after her last scan, when she was nearly sixteen weeks, she had a bleed at work. Nothing much, just a few spots, and not fresh blood, but a bleed for all that, and the bubble of happiness burst and brought her crashing down to earth. She stared at the blood, stark on her pale underwear, and gave up any pretence of courage.

Dan. She had to find Dan, but he'd left the ward, so she sent him a message and phoned Ben, and he sent her straight down for a scan. She messaged Dan again, and he and Ben made it just in time.

She was already lying there, top hitched up, trousers tugged down and her heart in her mouth when they arrived, and Dan stood beside her, her hand clenched in his as Steph scanned her, going carefully over every inch of the placenta, over the babies, the cords...

'Well, that all looks fine,' Ben said with a relieved smile, and they both started breathing again. 'They're both growing well and they're the same size, which is good. I'm happy with that.'

'So what caused it?' she asked.

'I have no idea, but I don't think it's anything to worry about. It's all looking good, but you need to take a couple of days off and rest, just to be on the safe side, and we'll go from there, but I'm pretty sure it's nothing. We just need to keep them in there until they're viable, and longer if possible.'

'So when would you deliver them by choice? Assuming they get to that point?' Dan asked.

'Any time from thirty-two weeks.'

'That's still so early,' she said.

'Not that early, we can deliver them any time from twenty-four weeks onwards if we really can't avoid it, but by thirty-two weeks they'll be safer out than in if we have any worries. If we don't, we might leave them to cook another week or two. But since you have had a bleed, I'm a little concerned about you living alone.'

'She isn't,' Dan said firmly. 'We're together.'

Which made it sound much more than it was, but it seemed to satisfy Ben. 'Good. And in the meantime I want you to have a 4D scan so we have a video of how they move and relate to each other. Some are more active than others. Have you felt them moving yet?'

'I'm not sure,' she said. 'I did wonder yesterday, but I put it down to wind. It's quite early.'

'It's not unheard of, and they're certainly

moving well, so it could be. Anyway, at the moment you're OK, they're OK and it's looking good for now, so I'm happy.'

True to his word, Ben had her scanned with monotonous frequency, and he was happy with her progress. Dan wasn't. Like Georgie, he was living on a permanent knife-edge. The stress in the build-up to each scan was hell to deal with, and every time it was all right he relaxed again. Until the next time.

They got to know the babies' faces in the 3D scan, watched them grow and develop over the next few weeks, and inevitably with all the scans there was no hiding the fact that they were girls, and of course that hit a nerve.

Would knowing they were boys have been any better? He wasn't sure. Either way losing them would break his heart, and the slow passage of every day was agonising, but bit by bit they got closer to viability.

Then when she was twenty weeks Ben sent them to London for a 4D scan with his brother Matt, and they watched the video of them moving and it suddenly all seemed so much more real. Matt was more than happy with the babies, so they went out for dinner afterwards to celebrate and all the Christmas lights were on, and it felt oddly romantic, almost like some surreal date. Only of course it wasn't, and he kept having to remind himself of that.

They spent Christmas at work, because everyone else had children, but because there were no scheduled electives the workload was lighter with only three straightforward deliveries, and everyone loved a Christmas baby, so it was a good day.

And another day nearer. She was almost twenty-two weeks, and after twenty-eight it should be safer, but the suspense was killing him.

At the beginning of January, when she was twenty-three weeks pregnant, she had a message as she was on her way to work from Laura Stryker, to say she was in labour and en route to the hospital. She'd seen her the week before at Livvy's, and she'd thought at the time that Laura looked imminent.

Nice to know pregnancy hadn't clouded her judgement, but she just hoped they got their boy, so that Tom wouldn't pass on the Retinitis Pigmentosa gene that was gradually robbing him of his sight. They'd chosen not to find out, but she knew they'd regretted that decision and were desperate to know now.

Georgie met them at the desk and gave

Laura a little hug, then changed quickly and went to handover.

'Laura Stryker's just come in,' she told Jan. 'Can I have her, please? And she wants the birthing pool.'

'Of course. No lifting, though, so you be careful and get someone else in to help you if it's tricky to get her out. And use the hoist if she can't help herself. I don't want you doing anything risky.'

She went straight back to them, and found Laura rocking backwards and forwards, one hand on her back, the other clinging to Tom, and Georgie checked the time.

It eased off, and Laura looked up and met her eyes. 'Is the birthing pool free?' she asked, and Georgie nodded.

'Yes. Let's move you in there. It'll take a little while to fill, but there's no hurry and I need to have a look at you and see how you're doing.'

Well, as it turned out. Her contractions were coming every three minutes and she was already seven centimetres, so as soon as the pool was full and Georgie was happy with the temperature, Laura stripped off and climbed in, wearing just a little vest top that she could quickly pull out of the way after the baby was born.

'Oh, that feels so good,' she said with a sigh of relief, and she didn't talk again after that. The odd moan, a bit of shifting around to find a comfortable position, Tom's hands supporting her and rubbing her back firmly during contractions while soft music played in the background.

Georgie checked her again when she came out to use the bathroom an hour later, and her cervix was fully dilated.

'You're doing really well. Want to go back in for the delivery?'

Laura nodded and climbed back into the water, sinking under it with a sigh of relief, then she gave a guttural groan and rolled over, kneeling up with her arms folded on the edge of the pool and pushing, and while Tom murmured gentle words of encouragement, Georgie pressed the button for another midwife and went round to the other side of the pool where she could keep an eye on her progress.

'OK, Laura, the baby's head's crowning, so nice little pants now, no more pushing, just let it happen,' she said, wondering where the other midwife was. Surely they weren't all busy?

They were, and she got Dan instead.

'You again. Having a career change?' she murmured with a smile, and he chuckled quietly and hunkered down beside her.

'Liv's on her way. Anything I can do?'

'Yes, turn the lights down a little more and get a towel ready in case we need to lift them out quickly, but I don't think we will. Here we go... Lovely, Laura, well done, tiny little push—OK, the head's out, so stay well under water and turn over—that's it. Well done.'

She was there beside her now, and as Laura gave one final push Georgie reached down into the water and lifted the baby up and out, so its head was clear of the water as it took its first gasp of air. Tom had pulled her top out of the way, and the baby lay cradled on her chest, blinking up at them in the gentle light.

'Hello, baby,' Laura said softly, but Tom's face was tense.

'What is it?' he asked, his voice tight, and Georgie moved the baby a fraction so she could see, and smiled up at them.

'It's a boy,' she said, her eyes filling with tears, and Tom's face crumpled.

'Oh, thank God,' he said, and he buried his face in Laura's shoulder and wrapped his arms around them both and sobbed with relief.

There was a tap on the door and Liv Jarvis came in. 'Oh, I've missed it!'

Georgie looked up and grinned at her. 'Still plenty to do.'

Dan gave a soft chuckle. 'Over to you,' he

murmured to Liv, congratulated the happy family and left them to it.

She was soaked by the time Laura was out of the water and dried, so as soon as the placenta was delivered she left Liv in charge and went to change, a little bubble of happiness inside her for them and their new son.

The babies were busily kicking her in the bladder, so she needed a quick wee and some dry scrubs, and then she'd be back in there to finish off the paperwork and settle Laura into a bed.

Except she didn't make it back, because she realised, now she had time to think about it, that the babies were very active. Worryingly active, and she was only twenty-three weeks. It was still much too soon. Would they make it? She didn't know and she was swamped with fear, but she rang Dan, he rang Ben, and once again they met at the scan room.

'So what's going on?'

'I don't know. A lot of wriggling and tumbling about, and I'm just really worried about the cords. I was doing a delivery, and then I realised how active they were—much more than usual.'

'OK, let's have a look.'

Yet again they watched as Steph scanned

her meticulously, checking the placenta for any issues, the cords for entanglement, the babies for any sign they might be distressed, but she found nothing of any major concern.

Ben took them into his office and sat them down.

'Right, I don't think this activity is significant, not this time, and they're quieter now and the cords aren't tangled, so I want you to chart the movements as you've been doing and we'll review it daily and if necessary we can deliver them if the situation changes.'

'It's too early,' she said, her hands instinctively going to her bump. 'They're not really viable, Ben. Not yet. They're so tiny.'

He nodded slowly. 'It's not ideal, I agree, but they're looking well, and they stand a chance now.'

'I want more than a chance!' she said desperately.

'I know. And I realise how tough this is for you both, but if we can keep you going then every day that passes makes a difference.'

'You're not going to put me on bed rest, are you?' she said, dreading his answer, and he shook his head.

'Not now, and probably not at all if it all proceeds well, but I want you on light duties only now, Georgie. I'll talk to Jan. Clinics only, shorter hours, less running around. If we can keep your workload down to a minimum but keep you here, that's the safest place.'

'Do you really think she should be at work?' Dan chipped in, his voice tight with worry, and she reached out and took his hand, as much for her own reassurance as for his.

'I don't think it'll hurt, but you certainly aren't doing any more deliveries. We can monitor you frequently during the day as you get further on, and once you've got past twenty-eight weeks or so the danger from entanglement doesn't seem to be the issue we once thought it was, so inpatient bed rest and monitoring doesn't seem as necessary as it did and doesn't have a measurable effect on the outcome. So, no, in short, we won't put you on bed rest unless it's absolutely necessary, but you'll be even more intensively monitored from now on. Don't worry, Georgie. We're keeping a very close eye on you and we'll act as soon as we think it's necessary.'

They walked out of Ben's office and Dan glanced at his phone.

'You need to talk to Jan, and I need to see how my registrar's doing and make sure Patrick hasn't lost the plot, and then how about lunch?'

Lunch? She was still in a bit of a daze, but actually… 'Yeah, why not? That's a great idea. It's a lovely sunny day. We can sit in the window of the Park Café and look at the trees. I'll call you.'

She went and found Liv, and she met her eyes and mouthed, 'You OK?' and Georgie nodded.

'Sort of. Had a bit of a hiccup with the babies. They were really active but I've had a scan, it's all OK, Ben's happy, but I'm going for lunch with Dan if you're able to carry on?'

'Yes, I'm fine. They're doing well. Utterly besotted, both of them. That baby's going to be so spoilt.'

'Like you'd never spoil your two,' she said with a smile, and after a quick word with Laura and Tom she left them to it and messaged Dan to tell him she'd see him in the café.

She went down in the lift because she felt suddenly exhausted, and by the time Dan got to the café she could hardly keep her eyes open. He slid into the seat opposite her and took her hand.

'You OK?'

'Tired. So, so tired. I think I'm just emotionally exhausted.'

'Well, not to mention the physical challenge.

You need fuel. Stay there, I'll get you something. What do you want?'

'I don't know. Get what looks nice.'

He did. He brought lasagne and a chicken casserole and gave her the choice, and she took the casserole, tasty and filling and full of healthy calories, and almost inhaled it, then sat back with a sheepish smile.

'Gosh, I needed that. Thank you.'

He gave a soft huff of laughter and finished his lasagne, drained his coffee and checked the time.

'Do you need to be somewhere?'

Another laugh. 'Always. It's not critical, I've got ten minutes. Want anything else?'

'An apple turnover for later? I'm so hungry these days.'

'Another one? I need to start feeding you more.'

'No, you don't, I'm going to be carrying enough weight…'

Her face must have changed, because he frowned and reached out a hand and took hers, squeezing it gently.

'You'll be OK,' he said, and she met his eyes and shook her head.

'You can't say that. You know you can't say that. You're a doctor, Dan. Don't promise what you can't deliver. That's the first rule. Don't tell people it'll be OK when you have no control over it. We have no control over this. We just have to wait it out.'

He squeezed her hand again. 'I know. I'm sorry. I just…'

'Want to make it all right?' She squeezed his hand back. 'I know. I understand.' She glanced up at the clock on the wall. 'Shouldn't you be going?'

'What about your cake?'

She shook her head. 'I don't need it. I've got biscuits in the ward kitchen. They'll do. I'll walk back with you. I need to find out what Jan's going to let me do for the rest of the day. If I know her, not a lot.'

They went back in together, and as they parted at the desk he dropped a kiss on her cheek and walked away, and she turned back to see Jan smiling.

'He's a nice man,' she said, and Georgie was on the point of opening her mouth and changed her mind, nodding instead.

'Yes, he is.' Even though he wasn't hers and never would be. She stifled the pang and smiled at Jan. 'So, what am I doing? Don't tell me, auditing the notes to find some spurious data that nobody really needs?'

Jan raised an eyebrow. 'I have no idea what you mean. The files are there. Go through them and see if you can spot any inconsistencies, anything that we could be doing better, or any patterns emerging that concern you.'

'Really?'

'Really,' Jan said firmly, and left her to it.

CHAPTER NINE

SHE GOT HOME before him—her house, because he was still at work and she'd be closer if the movements got too lively again.

She made herself a drink and propped herself up on the sofa, but it wasn't as comfortable as his and she was fidgety and restless.

Like the babies. Maybe if she went and lay down, it would be better. She climbed the stairs, shocked at how much harder it was now at only twenty-three weeks. She looked as if she were thirty weeks or more, so heaven knows what she'd look like by the time she reached thirty-four.

If she ever did.

She paused and closed her eyes, taking a moment to ground herself, then went on up, turned back the duvet and lay down on her side, her hand resting on her bump, feeling the movement of the babies. The crazy jiggling of earlier had gone, and they were peaceful now, just the odd wriggle or stretch.

'Please be OK, babies,' she murmured. 'I couldn't bear it if you weren't…'

She squeezed her eyes shut, but a great wrenching sob tore itself out of her chest, and she turned her face into the pillow and sobbed her heart out.

She was crying.

He could hear her the moment he came through the door, and he ran upstairs and found her on her bed, her hand splayed protectively over the babies.

He kicked off his shoes and lay down beside her, his hand finding hers and splaying over it.

'What's up?' he asked softly, and she lifted her head and met his eyes.

'I'm just so scared for them,' she said, her voice clogged with tears, and he eased her into his arms and pressed a kiss to her forehead.

'I know, but Ben's taking really good care of you, and he knows what he's doing.'

'He can't change fate.'

'No, but he can pre-empt it. He's doing a great job, and so are you. You can't do any more than that.'

She let out a shaky sigh and nodded. 'I know. I'm just being silly.'

No sillier than him. He'd struggled all day with this latest reminder of how fragile her pregnancy was, how quickly it could turn to disaster. But she didn't need to know that.

'Let's go back to mine, and I'll cook you a nice meal and we can watch something silly on the TV—a rom-com or something.'

She tilted her head back and looked at him. 'Really? A rom-com? That doesn't sound like you.'

'I like a rom-com. Why not?'

She smiled, in spite of herself, and rolled away from him. 'OK. Let's go,' she said, wriggling her feet back into her shoes and standing up slowly because her blood pressure was low and she got dizzy.

'OK?'

'Yup. Rom-com here we come.'

He sat her down on the sofa while he cooked, and when he called her through there were candles on the table.

'Gosh, that's a bit OTT for a weeknight,' she said with a smile, but he just grinned.

'Getting into the mood for the film,' he said, and brought their plates to the table. A delicious monkfish and roasted tomato penne, with a tiny kick of chilli—Italian food, in keeping with the romance, followed up by a light and delicate lemon dessert served in a dainty cup with an amaretto biscuit on the side.

She all but licked out the cup, then pushed it away. 'That was delicious, Dan. Thank you.'

His smile was gentle. 'You're welcome. Right, let's go and choose a film.'

They curled up on the sofa side by side, but then somehow she ended up lying with her head on his lap, with his arm around her and his hand splayed over her bump. Every now and again the babies would move, and his hand would stroke soothingly over them and they'd go back to sleep.

It wasn't long before she joined them, and she was woken by the click of the TV turning off.

'Time for bed,' he murmured, and she stretched and sighed and shook her head.

'Too comfy.'

'Tough,' he said with a chuckle, and shifted out from under her and pulled her slowly to her feet and into his arms.

It felt so right, so natural, and when they reached the bedroom door she stopped and met his eyes.

'Stay with me,' she said softly, and she saw something flicker in his eyes. 'Not—for that.

Just…' She had no idea what he was thinking, but in the end he nodded.

'OK—but in my room. The bed's bigger.'

Why did he agree?

It was every kind of torture, but he wouldn't have changed it for the world. They didn't make love. That wasn't what she needed, and it would have been a bad idea on every level, not least for her pregnancy. But lying with her head on his chest and her leg over his, he could feel the babies move and he knew they were all right.

Not so his arm, but then she rolled away and he winced and rubbed the life back into it, then curled in behind her, his arm draped over her waist and his hand on the babies, and gradually he fell asleep.

They slept together every night from then onwards, and she slept better than she had since the start of her pregnancy.

The weeks passed slowly, and with every check, their babies were that bit nearer to being viable. She wasn't sure how Dan felt about them being girls. Boys might have been better, but maybe the fact that they were girls was just more bittersweet. But he'd never mentioned it, and throughout it all he was wonderful.

Endlessly supportive, kind, funny—if it hadn't been for the fact that he was only doing it because of guilt and to keep his tiny girls safe, she could almost have believed they had a future.

Not that she dared to let herself think about it, because if the babies died, this would all stop. There'd be no need for him to look after her, no need for him to stay with her and hold her while she slept, no need for him to be with her at all, but as it was they were still taking one day at a time and she was doing her best not to be too needy or dependent.

She couldn't let that happen, because letting herself love him would be a recipe for disaster. They weren't together in that way, and never would be, and her pregnancy was still balanced on a knife-edge.

But even so, he was house-hunting.

He'd sold his house in Bristol and was looking for a three or four bedroomed house with a garden. She told him he was jumping the gun, don't tempt fate, pushing their luck, so he didn't go and view any, but he was still searching, and she wasn't sure how he would cope if anything happened to the babies now.

She passed the magic twenty-four-week viability milestone, then the twenty-eight-week one, then thirty—and then it was thirty-two and Ben was talking about delivering her, so she was started on steroids to mature the babies' lungs.

She had a bit of cord entanglement. Not enough to worry about, but enough that she was being monitored even more closely. She had a Doppler scan three times a day, and Dan was doing it morning and evening as well, and she was still doing the movement chart, sitting down for an hour and counting the number of movements in that time.

There were usually in excess of twenty-five, but sometimes more and sometimes hardly anything. They seemed to sleep most often when she was busy, and wake up when her pelvis was no longer rocking them with every stride and sending them off to sleep, so every time she lay down a football match would start.

And then one day towards the end of March, when she was thirty-four weeks and her section was scheduled for the next day, one of them went quiet.

She was at work, sitting at a desk uploading patient notes in the antenatal clinic, and it just felt—wrong.

And it was Dan's clinic.

She tapped on his consulting room door and

put her head round, and he beckoned her in, took one look at her face and ended his call.

'What?'

'They've been really active, lots of shoving and pushing, and now the one on the right isn't moving as much. It feels—odd.'

'Right. Scan, now,' he said, and as they walked the few steps to the ultrasound room, he was on the phone to Ben.

Steph was just finishing off, and the moment the couple came out they were in there. Ben arrived as Steph started to scan her, and together they studied the images.

She'd been right to worry. One of them had turned round, the cords were really tangled, and the baby on the right had the cord looped around her neck. It wasn't tight, and the heartbeats were similar, and she was moving a little more again now, but if either of them turned the wrong way she could die. It was seriously bad news, and she knew what Ben would say before he opened his mouth.

'Sorry, Georgie, we can't leave them like this, we'll have to do your section now. When did you last eat?'

'Breakfast,' she said, feeling giddy with fear and anticipation.

'Good, because I don't want to wait, it's too risky, so I need to put you under. I'm really sorry but it's the safest thing to do. If they move again…'

She nodded, and then found herself in a wheelchair being whisked up to Theatre. Her scrubs were peeled off, she was gowned and Peter, the anaesthetist, got the cannula in ready.

Dan was with her, holding her other hand, stroking the hair back off her face, and she could feel the tremors running through him, feel his fear, his dread, the storm of emotion that was going on inside him, but he was there with her, and she loved him for that.

'You'll be OK, Georgie,' he was saying. 'You'll all be OK. I'm here for you.'

They were the last words she heard as she slipped into unconsciousness.

'Are you coming in?' Ben asked through the doorway, but Dan's heart was pounding, adrenaline coursing through his body, and he thought he was going to throw up.

He shook his head. 'I'm sorry, I can't. I can't do this again. I can't lose anyone else. Just— don't let them die, Ben. For God's sake, don't let them die.'

Ben's eyes held a thousand questions, but he didn't have the words to explain and Ben didn't have time to listen. He took a step back, then another, and turned on his heel and strode out of Theatre, out past the lifts, down the stairs and out into the park, sucking in lungsful of air.

Please don't let them die. Don't let them die. Don't let them die...

He sank down under a tree and leant against it, staring blindly out across the park. He felt sick. He should be up there with Georgie, not down here wallowing in self-indulgence. He was such a coward. He should have been with her.

He buried his face in his hands, and then he felt a touch on his shoulder and looked up.

Patrick, hunkering down beside him, concern in his eyes.

'Are you OK, Mr Blake?'

He just laughed at that, but the laugh caught in his chest and came out as a sob. 'Georgie's in Theatre,' he said.

'I heard. So why aren't you there? She needs you.'

He shook his head. 'I can't. I can't do it again. I've been here before, and I can't—I just—'

'Yes, you can. Come on, Dan. Get up. I'll come with you. You're not alone, I'm here. Come on.'

He sucked in a huge breath, let it out again

slowly and got to his feet, then made his way back inside, Patrick beside him all the way. Patrick, the junior doctor who'd nearly driven him insane, and who now had come of age and found his strength.

There were seats outside the theatres, the seats where he'd left Rob on his first day, waiting to find out if Susie and the baby would survive.

Like the seats where he'd sat waiting for a cry from his baby, the cry that had never come.

'Sit down, Dan,' Patrick said gently, and he sat beside him, a hand on his shoulder, and they waited. Then Patrick's pager went off and he had to leave, and Dan felt lost without him there.

He didn't know how long he'd sat there staring at the door before it opened and a nurse came out. Ten minutes? An hour?

'Mr Blake? Your babies are with the NICU team, they're working on them but they're doing well, and Mr Walker's just closing. He said to tell you they're all OK.'

He closed his eyes, squeezing back the tears, but they fell anyway, tears of joy, disbelief, regret that he hadn't been there, guilt because his other baby had never had this chance. He had no idea how long he sat there as emotion ripped its way through him, wave after wave of pent-up feelings finally finding their release, until in the end he felt an arm around his shoulders, a solid shoulder to cry on.

Ben, who'd been there for them from start to finish, who'd saved his babies and his beloved Georgia, was there with him, saying nothing but offering his silent support.

He pulled away from him, hauled in a breath and scrubbed his hands over his face, and Ben handed him a tissue.

'Sorry. It's—it's been a hell of a pregnancy,' he said, and then he saw a glitter in Ben's own eyes as he smiled.

'I know. Congratulations. I'm so glad it's turned out so well for you both,' he said, his voice a little unsteady, and Dan laughed and hugged him hard.

'Thank you. Thank you so much. You have no idea what it means to me.'

'My pleasure. She's in Recovery now, and the babies are about to go up to NICU soon. Let me take you through so you can see them before they go.'

'Georgie? Georgia, I'm here.'

She opened her eyes and looked up at him, and his face swam into focus. His eyes were red-rimmed, his lashes clumped with tears, but he was smiling with every part of his face, and she was so happy to see him.

'Ben said they're alive,' she said with a little sob of joy. 'They're both alive.'

'I know. I've just seen them. They're beautiful, Georgie. So beautiful.' There were tears coursing down his cheeks, and his eyes were full of emotion as he put his arms around her and hugged her gently, her head cradled against his shoulder.

She could hardly believe they'd got so far. Their babies had made it against all the odds, and now it was down to the NICU staff to keep them safe.

Not quite out of the woods, but almost.

'Go and be with them,' she said to him tearfully. 'Tell them I'll come and see them as soon as I can. Tell them I love them.'

He nodded and got to his feet, then bent and kissed her.

'I love you, Georgia,' he said gruffly, and then he thanked Ben again and left, and Ben looked at her and winked.

'You OK?'

'I think so,' she said. 'Thank you so much.'

His eyes creased in a smile as broad as Dan's.

'It's my absolute pleasure. I couldn't be happier for you.'

But she hardly heard his words, because echoing in her head were Dan's last words before he'd gone.

'I love you...'

He hadn't meant to say that.

It had just come out, and it shocked him. Was it true? Did he love her? Actually, really *love* her? Like that?

Maybe. Possibly. He was certainly immensely proud of her, of the courageous way she'd coped with a complicated pregnancy that had had them both balanced on a knife-edge for weeks. And there was no doubt that he was attracted to her; even during the ordeal of this terrifying pregnancy she'd been beautiful to him, and he'd wanted her so much it had trashed his peace of mind and messed with his sleep. Until he'd had her in bed with him every night, and then it just felt right.

But—love?

He didn't think it was reciprocated.

She pushed him away at every turn, she'd accepted his help grudgingly because she was so fiercely independent, and she'd only done that out of common sense and pity for him because of his past.

No. That was unfair, and she was better than that. It was empathy, and her understanding of where he was coming from had made it easier, but she still hadn't cut him any slack if he helicoptered, as she put it. And being with her wasn't an easy ride. She was as sassy as hell, highly opinionated, knew her own mind and he didn't often win an argument. Although even that had been better recently, and she'd leant on him more and more as the weeks had crept by, but she was still fiercely independent.

So how could he love her, this contrary, awkward, prickly, defensive woman who'd fought her corner and stood up for herself against all odds?

How he could *not*? After all, she'd given him something he'd thought he'd never have. A family.

He watched through the glass as the NICU team worked on their babies. Wires, tubes, the endless beeping of machines were all around them. How would they cope with that?

And they were so tiny. So, so tiny. Well, not really. They were both just under two kilos, slightly over four pounds, and he'd delivered so many babies of that sort of weight who'd sailed through it, but these were *his*, his and Georgia's, and the sight of them, so small and so vulnerable, brought back all the painful memories that he'd tried so hard to subdue.

Memories of a baby who hadn't made it,

who'd weighed the same, who he'd held in his arms and loved with all his heart. He couldn't do that again. Please, let him not have to do that again.

Please let them live. Please let them be all right...

Someone was walking towards him, opening the door, smiling as she beckoned him in. 'Hi, Dan, I'm Sarah and I'm one of the team looking after your babies. Do you want to come in? They're all settled now.'

He nodded, and she checked his wristband, gave him a gown and a mask and led him over to the cot.

It wasn't the first time he'd been in there. He and Georgie had been given a guided tour a few weeks ago as it had been anticipated that the babies might need to be in here, but also he'd come up here to see Susie's baby on his first day, right after he'd left Georgie in her bed on the night their twins had been conceived.

He would never have imagined on that night that he'd end up being the father of a baby in here, never mind two, but there they were, alive and apparently doing well.

They were in a twin cot, lying side by side with their scrawny little arms touching, just as they had been all their lives to now. So close they were almost one. It brought a lump to his throat. And he had to swallow hard before he could speak.

'I'm so glad they can touch each other. They're so used to it. They've never been apart. I can't believe they're actually here, that they've made it this far.'

'No. They're pretty special babies.'

'Yes, they are.' He swallowed the lump again and pulled himself together. 'So which is which?' he said, staring down at two identical little faces, or what he could see of them with the tubes taped to their cheeks.

'The one on the left is twin number one, the one that had the cord around her neck, and the one on the right is twin two. Have they got names?'

He shook his head. 'No. We haven't talked about it yet.'

Hadn't dared, for fear of tempting fate, just like he hadn't bought a house yet, and they had no cots, no baby car seats, no buggy—nothing. Not even a packet of nappies, because she wouldn't hear of it until she knew they were OK. And as for names…

'We ought to do that,' he murmured, staring down at them in awe, watching their little chests rising and falling steadily.

'You might find it helps. Bonding with a

baby you can't hold or touch is very difficult, but giving them names somehow makes them seem more real, so people say.'

He nodded. His baby had never had a name, or not one he'd ever known, and that still broke his heart, but in his head she was Emily, because she'd just looked like an Emily.

'I'll talk to Georgia. She's probably got some ideas.'

They talked a bit longer, about the care they'd need, how long they'd be in there, how they were being fed, and then Sarah gave him a chair and left him there, and he sat beside them, staring through the clear walls of the cot, watching them breathe. That in itself was a miracle. He pulled out his phone and took a little video of them for Georgie, and as he was about to stop twin two stretched and yawned, and he didn't know whether to laugh or cry. He ended up with a bit of both, then after a while Sarah came back.

'Georgie's back on the ward and she's asking for you,' she said, and he nodded and got to his feet.

'You will let us know if anything changes?'

'Of course we'll let you know, and you can come back and see them any time you want to. We'll bring Georgie in here to see them later, once she's settled in her room. She's just down the corridor on the left.'

He took one last look at them and headed out to find her.

'Hi, you.'

She smiled at him. 'Hi.'

He came over to her and took her hand. 'How are you doing?'

She wasn't sure. She was still trying to work out if he'd actually meant what he'd said. 'I'm fine, but never mind me, how are the babies?'

'They're amazing. I took this for you.' His smile was a little crooked, and he perched on the edge of the chair by her bed and pulled out his phone and showed her a little video clip of them, and her eyes filled with tears.

'Oh! Oh, that's really sweet! I can't believe that little yawn. Which one is she?'

'The second. Twin two. They need names, Georgia. They should have names.'

There was something in his voice, and she looked up at him and caught a hint of sadness in his eyes. He'd never mentioned his baby by name. Maybe she'd never had one?

'Yes. Yes, they should,' she said gently, and then, 'Have you got any ideas?'

He looked a bit surprised at that. 'I thought you would.'

She shrugged. 'A few. I didn't really want to let myself think about it. Not until they were safely here.'

'No. I didn't either.' He settled back in the chair. 'So let's hear your thoughts, then.'

'I don't know. Should they start with the same letter? Should they be completely different?'

He chuckled softly. 'I don't think there are rules.'

'They need to go with Blake.'

'Or with Seton.'

'Seton-Blake?' she offered, and he smiled.

'That's quite a mouthful,' he said, and pulled out his phone. 'I think we might need help. Shall we start with the As?'

They worked through the list, and she was on the point of giving up when they reached the Es.

'Emily's nice,' she said, and his face froze.

'Not Emily,' he said.

He didn't say why, but he didn't need to. It was enough that he didn't want it, so she let it go. 'OK. Elizabeth? Eva?'

'They'd work together.'

'Put them on the shortlist, then,' she said, and they moved on, reaching the Is without any further consensus.

'India's interesting.'

'With what?'

He shrugged. 'Isla? Iona? Isabel?'

She shook her head. 'One of my friends has an Isabel and the others are all place names.'

He put his phone down and looked at her. 'D'you know what? I like Elizabeth and Eva. Beth and Evie. They all work with Seton-Blake.'

She smiled, liking the sound of them—and the sound of Seton-Blake. 'Yes, they do. Happy with that?'

'I think so, if you are. They're your babies.'

'No. They're *our* babies,' she said firmly, then added, 'I wonder when they'll let me see them?'

'Soon, I think. They're going to wheel you in there on the bed for a little while.'

She felt a shiver of excitement. 'I want to see them now.'

'Shall I go and ask?'

'Could you?'

It wasn't long enough, but then it never would be, she realised, because if she looked at them for ever she'd still struggle to believe that they were hers.

They were so beautiful, so tiny and per-fect and vulnerable, and yet they were ap-parently doing well. She could hardly bear to leave them, but Ben was on his way up to see her and they needed to be fed. Just a tiny bit, a few mils every hour, but they at least had names now.

Beth was the first one to be born, the one who'd had the cord around her neck, and Evie was the second, the one who'd obligingly yawned for their video, and when Georgie spoke their names they'd both turned their heads towards the sound.

'They recognise your voice,' Dan said, and she felt the comforting warmth of his hand as he squeezed her shoulder.

She nodded. 'They've heard enough of it for today. We need to leave them in peace,' she said, and as her bed was wheeled back out to her room she was swallowing back tears. She should be holding them, feeding them, being a mother instead of a post-op patient forced to take a back seat to the NICU team.

'Hey,' he said softly, taking her hand as the nurses left them. 'They're doing well. You'll soon be able to hold them.'

'I should be expressing my colostrum for them,' she said, wondering if they'd ever be able to breastfeed or if their reflexes would be dented by the ease of tube and then bottle feeding. Breastfeeding was hard work for prem babies, and lots of them failed to establish it.

Please let them make it.

She shut her eyes, but the tears slid down her cheeks anyway, and she felt Dan's arms around her, hugging her gently.

'Don't cry,' he murmured. 'They'll be all right.'

'You don't know that. Nobody knows that.'

'Hey, come on, chin up, they've got this far and they're doing well. Mop yourself up. Ben's here.'

She felt the soft touch of a tissue on her cheeks, and opened her eyes to find Ben standing at the foot of the bed watching them.

'How are you doing?' he asked, all matter-of-fact despite the warmth in his eyes, and she was glad he was there, glad he'd been there for all of them.

'I'm fine. Thank you so much for everything you've done for us.'

'Don't be daft, it's my job and I wasn't going to let you down, I'd never hear the end of it,' he said, brushing it aside. 'Let's have a look at your incision. I have to say I'm pretty proud of it.'

'Modest with it, aren't you?' she teased, and he grinned.

'No point in denying my genius,' he said, but behind the cocky grin was a kindness fathoms deep, and she knew how much of himself he'd invested in her care.

He was a good friend, and she was hugely grateful for all he'd done for them. Only apparently she wasn't allowed to tell him that, so she lay there and smiled as he checked her over, nodded in satisfaction at her wound under its dressing and covered her up.

'How's the pain level?'

She shrugged. 'It's quite sore now.'

'OK, first things first. We'll get you some pain relief, then get you out into a chair and see how you feel, and then you maybe need to think about feeding those babies, but the midwives will deal with all of that, and I'll come and see you again later.'

It was the third day before she could hold the babies in her arms, and it seemed like a year, but when the time came it was the most wonderful thing that she'd ever known.

They'd been able to lose the feeding tubes on the second day, and without the tape on their faces she started to be able to tell the difference between them. Beth was quieter, more watchful than Evie, and Evie was a bit more active, but they were breathing normally for themselves without supplementary oxygen.

And they were both hungry. They'd lost

weight, which was normal, but there was little enough of them so of course she worried. She was expressing her milk for them, but there wasn't much at first, and they were being topped up with donated breast milk, for which she was hugely grateful.

She was grateful for Dan, too.

He was back at work, but popping up all the time to check on her and his tiny daughters, saving his paternity leave for when she left hospital. He spent as much time as he could with them, but he didn't tell her again that he loved her.

He probably hadn't meant it, or at least in the way she'd rather hoped he had. Foolish, really. She knew he was only here for the little ones, she'd been reminding herself of that for months, and it was stupid to let herself believe otherwise.

Then her milk really came in, on the day that Beth had a minor setback and had to have a feeding tube again, and she hit the four-day blues with a vengeance.

Dan found her curled up on her bed, sobbing silently, and he sat down beside her and stroked a tendril of hair off her face and kissed her.

'Hey, you. Bad day?' he murmured, and she nodded.

'Beth's got a feeding tube again,' she said.

'I know, but she's doing OK. It's just a little setback, nothing major.' He hoped…

'I know. I'm just being stupid,' she said, and he smiled and hugged her gently.

'No, you're not, it's your hormones.'

She gave him a look through tear-clumped lashes. 'You do know if you say that to me under any other circumstances you're dead meat?' she said, and he chuckled.

'Fair enough, but for now at least it is true. You know what's going on. Why don't you mop yourself up and we'll go and see the girls together?'

She nodded, sniffed and scrubbed at her cheeks, and he handed her a tissue and helped her off the bed. She winced, and he frowned.

'Do you need more pain relief?'

'No, I'm fine, I just want to be able to go home with my babies.'

'I know. It won't be long. They're doing really well. Let's go and give them a cuddle.'

He put his arm round her and gave her a gentle hug, and then walked slowly with her through to NICU. She was leaning on him, but then she was leaning on him for so much these days that it was becoming a habit.

A habit she probably needed to wean herself off, because it wasn't for ever—was it?

But in her head was a persistent echo of his voice, saying, 'I love you.'

If only she dared to believe it.

CHAPTER TEN

TWO DAYS LATER Ben let her go home, and Dan stayed with her. Her mother had been for a flying visit to meet the babies, but she was unable to take time off from running her guest house at the start of the Easter holidays, and her father lived in New Zealand with his second wife and in any case didn't know one end of a baby from the other, so there was nobody who could be at home with her apart from Dan, and she didn't know what she would have done without him.

They were based at her house so they were closer to the hospital in case there was a problem with either of the babies, and he looked after everything. The food, the shopping—he even watered the plants which were starting to grow again.

He was back in her spare room, though, not in her bed as he had been for weeks now. He said it was because of her incision, but she thought it was probably because the babies were safe now and so his vigil wasn't necessary any more, but she missed his presence and her bed felt lonely and empty without him.

He was still at work because they wanted to preserve as much of his paternity leave as they could, and every morning he took her to the hospital and brought her home at the end of the day.

The babies had been moved out of NICU into the neonatal ward, and she spent most of her time either with them or attached to the breast pump, and someone—Livvy or Daisy, usually—would take her home in the middle of the day so she could rest for a while, then take her back, and gradually both she and they grew stronger.

They were gaining weight fast now, making huge progress, and by the time they would have been thirty-six weeks she was able to breastfeed them both when she was there. And on the eighteenth day after they were born, she was allowed to take them home.

His home.

Needless to say she'd protested, but his arguments were reasonable. His bedroom was bigger, which would allow more room for the cot, and as the weather was warmer she'd be able to sit out in the garden with them in the shade of the trees.

But it was Laura, living just around the corner with her little baby James, that clinched it for her. They'd be able to spend time together once Dan was back at work, and Livvy with her baby Esme was also within easy walking distance. She'd have Daisy, too, not far away, and she'd never been so grateful for the close community that had been forged in the hospital.

And anyway, it was only until she was properly back on her feet and the babies were in a sensible routine.

So she agreed, and the night before they were discharged he took her there so she could make sure she was happy that it was ready for them, and when she walked into his bedroom her eyes filled with tears.

He'd somehow, with very little spare time, built the hastily ordered cot and made it up with a freshly washed new sheet, and hung a lovely little mobile, a gift from Ben and Daisy, from the ceiling. There was a chest of drawers with a changing table on it, a comfy chair with low arms for breastfeeding, and in the drawers were all the tiny little clothes they'd need for the first few weeks, and his bed was made up all ready with fresh linen.

'I thought you and the babies would be better in here,' he said. 'But I won't be far away, just next door.'

'Next door?' she said, and she felt a wash of guilt that she'd turned him out of his room, the room they'd shared. But maybe that was how he wanted it.

'Happy with it?' he asked, and she nodded, even though she would have been happier with him in there with her, but that was being unrealistic, she realised. Time to get real.

'Very. It looks perfect. Thank you.'

'Don't thank me, they're my children too.'

They were, but it still seemed unfair.

'It feels so wrong to turn you out.'

'It's fine. We've agreed—and anyway, I haven't slept in here for ages, I've been at yours since they were born, and I can sleep anywhere. And besides, I've moved all my stuff.'

'If you're sure…'

'I'm sure,' he said firmly. 'Come on, let's take you home so you can pack your things ready for the morning and get an early night.'

She packed her clothes ready for the morning, which didn't take long as there wasn't much that fitted her now, then perched on a seat in her little garden while he made supper, wondering when she'd be here again.

The plants were starting to emerge from their winter rest, the leaves opening, small shoots pushing up out of the compost, and there'd be nobody there to water them. How would they survive?

'It's ready. Want to eat out here?' he asked, standing in the doorway, but it was getting chilly and she shook her head.

'No, it's too cold now. I'll come in.'

She gave it one last look and stepped inside, and he frowned and tipped her head up with a gentle finger under her chin. 'What's up?'

'My plants. They're all going to die, aren't they?'

'No,' he said, and then surprised her yet again. 'I've got a plan for them. I thought we could move them to mine and group them around the edge of the patio. I can look after them that way, and you'll be able to enjoy them.'

She gave a ragged little sigh. 'I don't know what I'd do without you,' she said, choked, and he gave her a crooked smile.

'I hate to state the obvious, but without me you wouldn't be in this situation.'

She wouldn't—and without him, she wouldn't have her beautiful little girls, either. She smiled and kissed his cheek. 'No, I wouldn't, would I? Shall we eat?'

* * *

'Is this everything?'

She nodded and followed him downstairs, taking one last lingering look at her bedroom before she left it. Had she just spent her last night here? She had no idea. She couldn't really afford anything bigger on her own, and Dan really wasn't part of that equation. Well, at least, she didn't think he was, although he'd talked a lot about houses. If only she could read his mind…

She closed the door, went downstairs and by the time she reached the bottom he'd stashed her bags in the boot of the car and he was waiting for her.

'All set?'

'What about the fridge?' she asked, but he'd already thought of that, as he'd thought of everything else. It was open, emptied, washed and left ajar to keep it aired, and everywhere was immaculate. Goodness knows what time he'd got up, or when he'd come to bed.

She had one last look at her sitting room, then closed the door on that, too.

It seemed oddly symbolic. Would she ever live here again? She wasn't sure, and even if she did, it wouldn't be the same. Nothing would ever be the same again.

She set the alarm, stepped outside and closed the door on her old life for ever.

They were escorted out of the hospital by a fleet of well-wishers, with Dan carrying Evie and Ben carrying Beth, strapped into their little car seats side by side, and as they drove away from the security of the hospital she felt a shiver of apprehension.

How would they cope? One would be hard enough, but two tiny babies who needed feeding every two hours—she was going to be on her knees. How would *she* cope? Because Dan couldn't breastfeed them, with the best will in the world.

He glanced across at her. 'Hey, stop worrying, it'll be fine.'

'Fine?' she said, and gave a hollow little laugh. 'It'll be hard, Dan, is what it'll be. And relentless.'

'Yes, it will, but it'll get easier.'

'Will it? I don't know. I think we'll just get used to it.'

If it doesn't break us first...

She closed her eyes and rested her head back, and after a few minutes she felt the car stop and he cut the engine.

'Hey, sleepyhead.'

She opened her eyes. 'I wasn't asleep, just...'

'Gathering yourself,' he said, and she realised he was doing that, too. Gathering himself for what was to come.

Please let it be all right.

He wouldn't let her lift a finger.

Probably just as well, because by the time
she'd fed them, which was the first and most
important thing, she was so tired she could
barely manage to drag herself upstairs to
change their nappies and settle them in the cot.

'Why don't you get ready for bed?' Dan said
softly. 'I'll give you a few minutes to get settled. Do you want a drink?'

'Oh, yes. Tea would be lovely, please,' she
said, and he nodded and ran lightly downstairs,
leaving her to undress.

He'd unpacked her clothes and put them
away for her, and to her surprise they were
all in a logical place. It shouldn't have surprised her, really, he was a very logical and
methodical person, and he always paid attention to detail.

It was one of his best and yet most irritating
features, she thought with a smile. She pulled
out a clean sleep bra and her cat nightie, mostly
because it was short so it would be easy to pull
up to feed them, but also because it was the
most comfortable.

When he came upstairs she was sitting on the edge of the bed looking at the babies, and he put the tea down and came and sat beside her and put his arm around her shoulders.

'You OK?' he asked softly, and she nodded.

'I can't believe we're here with them. I never thought we'd get to this point, not like this.'

'No, nor did I.'

His voice was sad, and she turned her head and looked at him, searching his eyes. 'I'm so sorry about your baby, Dan,' she said quietly. 'I didn't really understand until I had ours just what it would mean to lose them. No wonder your heart's broken.'

There was a flicker of his lips, not really a smile, and it didn't reach his eyes before he turned back to them. 'She looked so like they did when they were born. It was almost as if I'd been given her back.' He met her eyes again. 'I had a bit of a meltdown while you were in Theatre.'

'I know. Ben told me you'd said you couldn't do it again, couldn't lose anyone else, so I told him what had happened to you. I hope you don't mind?'

He shook his head. 'No, of course I don't mind. I'm glad you did, but I'm sorry I wasn't there for you. I felt really guilty about it, but I couldn't stay, I was in bits, and afterwards

I hated myself for abandoning you like that, for abandoning them, but I couldn't watch—'

'Hey, Dan, it's OK. It's OK. It must have been incredibly hard for you, the whole pregnancy.'

'It was, but looking at them now it was worth every single second of it. They're so precious.'

'They are.'

He took a deep breath, let it out slowly and smiled at her. 'I have an idea. You and the babies need to sleep, and we can't leave them alone, so I can lie in here with them and you can sleep in the other room until they need feeding again, if you like.'

'Or you could stay here with me,' she said softly, and for a moment neither of them moved a muscle.

'I'm not sure that's a good idea,' he said eventually, and she plastered on a smile and tried not to feel rejected. Of course he didn't want her. That wasn't what this was about.

'No. Probably not. There's no point in us both being exhausted.'

He frowned at her. 'I wasn't thinking of me, I was thinking of you.'

'Then stay,' she said. 'You can pick them up and give them to me when they need feeding, and you can change their nappies. You'll enjoy that—and you need the practice,' she added, just to lighten what seemed suddenly a very intimate moment.

Again he hesitated, then he gave a wry little smile and nodded. 'OK. Why don't you go first in the bathroom and I'll sort myself out and come and join you?'

They sat up in bed drinking their tea, and then he put his arm around her and gave her a hug.

'I'm so proud of you. That pregnancy must have been hell for you, but I never once heard you grumble or complain.'

'Oh, I did.'

'No. Not really. You just gritted your teeth and got on with it. I'm in awe.'

She tilted her head and looked up into his eyes, and he leant over slightly and kissed her. It was a chaste kiss, but filled with tenderness, and it gave her courage.

'There's something I want to ask you,' she said quietly.

'Well, two things, really, but the second one might not be relevant.'

'Why don't you start with the first, then?'

'I'm not sure I want to. I'm not sure I'm brave enough, because if the answer's no, it'll spoil everything, and I know it's not really what you want anyway.'

'Spit it out, Georgia. The suspense is killing me.'

But he was smiling, and she didn't want that to end, so she took a mental photo of it before she ruined it all.

'I might start with the second one. I was thinking, we've been living together for months now, sort of, and—well, now we've got the babies, it might be really rather nice if we kept that going.'

'I thought we were.'

'But—only for now.'

'It doesn't have to be. I didn't think you'd want more,' he said, and she searched his eyes.

'So what do you want?'

He smiled again. 'I want to know what the first question was.'

'Oh.' She looked away, her heart picking up, and took a deep breath. 'When I was in Recovery, you said you loved me. Did you mean it?'

'Yes. Yes, I did. Did you want me to?'

She nodded, feeling a warmth spreading inside her. 'Yes, I did, because I love you, too. I didn't want to, because I thought you didn't want a relationship.'

'No. I didn't want to be in a position again where I could be so vulnerable to hurt, to loss, but that was rather taken out of our hands. And the more I've got to know you, the more I've grown to love you, even though you pushed me away as hard as you could.'

'Only to protect us both.'

He laughed softly. 'Yeah. We should have thought of that earlier, but I can't tell you how glad I am that we didn't.' His smile faded, and he became all serious. 'You asked me what I wanted, and I think you've just given me the answer, so I have a question for you now. Will you marry me, Georgia Seton?'

'Ma—?' She sucked in a breath. 'Oh, Dan. Really? Do you mean that? It's not just because of the babies? Because the last thing I want is someone pretending that they love me—'

'I'm not pretending, Georgia. I wouldn't pretend about something as important as that. I want to marry you, to live with you, and bring up our babies here, in this house, together.'

She felt her eyes widen. 'Here? But—I thought you were going to buy somewhere?'

'I am.' He looked a bit guilty. 'I didn't discuss it with you first because I wasn't sure what you'd say and you didn't want to talk about it, but I've spoken to Tom, and he might be willing to sell it to us. It'll need extending of course, in time, but if that was done sympathetically we could have a lovely house with plenty of room for—'

'Yes.'

He stopped talking and looked hard at her, and then he started to smile. 'Yes, it'll need extending?'

She started to laugh. 'No, you idiot, although it will. I mean yes, I'll marry you. I'll marry you,' she said again, the laughter gone, replaced by total and utter conviction. 'I love you, Daniel Blake, more than I could ever have imagined, and I'd be honoured to be your wife.'

He swallowed hard, drew her gently back into his arms and kissed her. She could feel all the pent-up love and tenderness that he poured into it, and when he lifted his head his eyes were brim-full of emotion, with a touch of humour.

'I can't believe you said yes without arguing. You've just made me the happiest man alive, Georgia Seton-Blake.'

She looked into his eyes. 'You can't call me that yet,' she said, and he smiled that lazy, sexy smile that made her heart turn over.

'Just practising...'

* * * * *